Praise for Arlene James

"Warm, rich details combine with Southern charm and hospitality in this touching story about healing deep emotional wounds."
—*RT Book Reviews* on *Second Chance Match*

"Arlene James has an exquisite way with words and… the characters and intricate plot will resonate long after the last page is turned."
—*RT Book Reviews* on *To Heal a Heart*

"Ms. James's multilayered characters, along with a richly textured story line, takes the reader on an emotional roller-coaster that will have you reaching for the nearest tissue."
—*RT Book Reviews* on *Mr. Right Next Door*

Praise for Lois Richer

"Lois Richer delivers a touching, evocative, wonderful story of selfless love."
—*RT Book Reviews* on *A Cowboy's Honor*

"A wonderful, emotionally heartwarming story about loss and love."
—*RT Book Reviews* on *Twice Upon a Time*

"Lois Richer pens an excellent story."
—*RT Book Reviews* on *Spring Flowers, Summer Love*

Arlene James has been publishing steadily for nearly four decades and is a charter member of RWA. She is married to an acclaimed artist, and together they have traveled extensively. After growing up in Oklahoma, Arlene lived thirty-four years in Texas and now abides in beautiful northwest Arkansas, near two of the world's three loveliest, smartest, most talented granddaughters. She is heavily involved in her family, church and community.

Lois Richer loves traveling, swimming and quilting, but mostly she loves writing stories that show God's boundless love for His precious children. As she says, "His love never changes or gives up. It's always waiting for me. My stories feature imperfect characters learning that love doesn't mean attaining perfection. Love is about keeping on keeping on." You can contact Lois via email, loisricher@gmail.com, or on Facebook (loisricherauthor).

Christmas
on the Ranch

Arlene James

&

Lois Richer

HARLEQUIN® LOVE INSPIRED®

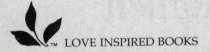 LOVE INSPIRED BOOKS

Recycling programs
for this product may
not exist in your area.

ISBN-13: 978-0-373-21444-0

Christmas on the Ranch

Copyright © 2017 by Harlequin Books S.A.

The publisher acknowledges the copyright holders
of the individual works as follows:

The Rancher's Christmas Baby
Copyright © 2017 by Deborah Rather

Christmas Eve Cowboy
Copyright © 2017 by Lois M. Richer

This edition published by arrangement with Love Inspired Books.

® and TM are trademarks of Love Inspired Books, used under license. Trademarks indicated with ® are registered in the United States Patent and Trademark Office, the Canadian Intellectual Property Office and in other countries.

www.Harlequin.com

Printed in U.S.A.

CONTENTS

THE RANCHER'S CHRISTMAS BABY

Arlene James

Blessed are those who find wisdom,
those who gain understanding.
—*Proverbs* 3:13

Chapter One

"Sorry, Dad," Dixon said into his cell phone. "You've got to get the plumber back in here before I can set these kitchen cabinets. Water's running down the outside of this pipe." Dixon listened to the expected complaints. He shared his father's frustration. They'd hoped to have this old house completely renovated before Thanksgiving and rented by the end of November, but the first week of December had now come and gone, and the kitchen cabinets weren't even installed.

Dixon blamed himself. Carpentry wasn't his only occupation, and not since he'd inherited his maternal grandfather's small ranch some eight years earlier had he experienced so much sickness in his herd as recently. These days it seemed he was constantly leaving the job to tend to some ailing cow. He had an injured heifer in the barn now, and he might as well get home to take care of it because he sure wasn't going to get anything more done here today.

Fitting his brown beaver cowboy hat to his head, he briefly considered stopping in at the War Bonnet diner for an early dinner, but he was more tired of the diner's meager offerings than he was hungry. Not that he had many choices. Like many small towns in Oklahoma, little War Bonnet's options were severely limited. He decided he'd open a can at home. After all, he'd worked long and hard to update the kitchen in the 1970s-era ranch house. Might as well make use of it.

The hour hadn't reached 5:00 p.m. when he turned his pickup truck onto the red dirt drive of the home place, but it was dark enough to see that he'd left lights on in the house. That wasn't like him. He'd lived alone since before his twenty-first birthday and had learned long ago what it took to keep the utility bills in line with the budget. At just weeks shy of his twenty-ninth birthday, he prided himself on his ability to budget and manage his money. He wouldn't have been able to remodel the house otherwise, let alone invest in rental property.

As he drew closer, he saw a small, battered, dark-colored sedan parked in front of the house. Obviously, he had a visitor, someone who felt they didn't have to wait on the front veranda but could just go inside and make themselves at home. It had never occurred to him to lock up the place, even after he'd remodeled, painting the orange brick white and replacing the dark shingles on the low roof with red metal. The house had a Spanish flair now, which he felt suited the long, lean lines, with a red front door and red shutters flanking the wide front windows.

Dixon couldn't imagine who would let themselves into his house. Unless... But

surely not. She'd left right after Dixon's eigh-
teenth birthday and had been back only for
Grandpa Crane's funeral. He hadn't seen her
in over eight years. Some letters had come,
none of which he'd answered, and he'd taken
a few short calls from her, but that had been
it. Must be two or more years since he'd last
heard a peep from Jackie.

Still puzzled, he pulled his truck into the
inner bay of the carport that he'd added to
the end of the house after he'd converted the
garage into a game room. The new parking
placement allowed him to quietly enter the
house via a mudroom off the kitchen. Still
wearing his tan canvas coat and brown felt
hat, he carefully walked to the kitchen door,
which had been pushed aside on its trendy
barn door rolling hinge.

At his stainless-steel stove stood a petite
young woman with warm brown skin and
very long, ink-black hair caught at her nape
by a big silver clasp. She wore brown suede
boots, plain, snug jeans and a simple top of
black knit with pushed-up sleeves, a belt of

silver links riding low on her slender hips. As if sensing his presence, she suddenly turned. On some level he registered the baby snuggled in the bend of her left arm, but a far larger part of his consciousness reeled in shock at the sheer perfection of her face. From the delicate roundness of her chin and the dusky rose of her lips to the straight line of her nose, the piercing blackness of her exotic eyes and the gentle slashes of her brows beneath the sweep of thick hair that framed all that loveliness from a loose, haphazard center part.

"Hello," she said, but he was too dumbfounded to return the greeting. She tilted her head, studying him as if he were a bug pinned in a display case. He wanted to feel his jaw to see if he needed a shave, but of course he needed a shave; he'd last taken care of the chore before daylight and despite his medium brown hair, he had an unusually heavy beard. By the end of most workdays, he looked like a vagrant.

A movement to his right pulled his attention toward the breakfast nook, where a tall, painfully thin woman slid around the corner to lean against the wall. Her dark blond hair, streaked liberally with gray, had been pulled back from her face in an apparent attempt to disguise its thinness. She looked familiar, but she had so many lines in her face that he didn't immediately recognize her. Then she gave him that saucy grin, showing off the false teeth that he remembered her husband, Harry, had bought her to help hide the ravages of her meth addiction, and he knew without a shadow of a doubt what he had been trying not to see. Jackie. The very last person he wanted to find in *his* house. Grandpa Crane's will had made it very clear that she had no claim to ownership.

"I really like what you've done with the place," she said in a husky voice, glancing around the room.

Dixon sighed and got right to the heart of the matter.

"What are you doing here, *Mother*?"

* * *

"Well, that's a nice greeting," Jackie said, managing to toss her head.

"You expected a parade?" he asked.

"*Some* welcome would be nice."

"Some *notice* would've been nice."

Listening to this exchange, Fawn bounced the baby gently and reached for the bottle she'd been preparing. Dixon Lyons was not what she'd expected. He was more man than boy, though Jackie constantly referred to him as "my boy." Also, he was amazingly attractive. She didn't know why she'd never considered that possibility, but her concern for Jackie and the baby was so great that she hadn't stopped to think about anything other than Dixon's willingness to accept them into his home, and a lovely home it was. Jackie hadn't stopped talking about all the improvements he'd made or what good taste he had—until he'd arrived. Now the woman had suddenly become defensive and snide, not at all like the brave, stoic Jackie whom Fawn knew.

"Uh, you did say that Dixon was unaware of Harry's passing," Fawn reminded her older friend. At that, Jackie bowed her head.

"Something happened to Harry?" Dixon asked, sounding both concerned and shocked.

Jackie nodded, wobbling slightly. "Highway accident."

"I'm sorry. I didn't know. When did it happen?"

"Almost eight months ago."

"Eight…" He lifted his hat and ran a hand over his short, thick hair. "And you're just now letting me know because…?"

"It's been a difficult time," Jackie muttered, swaying on her feet.

Fawn hurried over and pulled out a chair at the round table with her right hand. "Sit down before you fall down." Like most of the furniture in the house, the dinette was older but of good quality.

Jackie sank down onto the chair just as Dixon glanced at Fawn. "Maybe my mother and I should speak in private."

"No," Jackie insisted. "Fawn has a stake

in this conversation." She smiled wanly. "If not for her, I wouldn't be here."

"I'm Fawn Ambor, by the way," Fawn introduced herself, holding out her right hand. Dixon merely glanced at her then at the baby before turning back to his mother. As if realizing she had been snubbed, the baby started to fuss.

"Give her to me," Jackie said, holding out her thin arms. Not even the long sleeves of her cotton blouse could disguise her frailness.

"No, no. You rest a few more minutes," Fawn said. "I'll take care of her."

Jackie nodded and pushed up from her chair. "Maybe you're right. I do feel weak."

Fawn went to get the bottle and give it to the whimpering baby.

"So what happened?" Dixon asked, coming to lean against the rust-and-gold granite countertop. "Harry throw her out before the accident?"

Fawn turned to find Jackie standing, stiff-backed, in the wide, cased doorway. "No! Why would you think that?"

Dixon didn't so much as glance in his mother's direction. "She's back here, isn't she?"

Lifting her chin, Jackie slowly made her way into the other room. Fawn leaned closer, holding the baby to the side, and demanded softly, "Are you always so disrespectful of your mother?"

"She's never given me any reason not to be," he answered bluntly.

"She gave birth to you," Fawn told him. "That should be reason enough."

"Yeah, well, you weren't here when she was the talk of the town, running off to any-where and everywhere she could find a party and her drug of choice."

"No, I wasn't here then," Fawn conceded softly, "but did you ever ask yourself why your mother did those things?"

He lifted a rather heavy eyebrow, his clear gray eyes coldly impassive. "Little boys don't ask why their mothers are zonked-out druggies. Instead, they blame themselves. Until they grow up and figure out personal responsibility."

Slapping his hat onto his head, he walked out through the same door from which he'd entered. Shaken, Fawn turned and followed Jackie from the room. She found her friend snuggled into an oversize armchair in front of the cold fireplace, a fuzzy blanket over her legs.

"Think you can hold her while she nurses?" Fawn asked, handing the baby and bottle down to Jackie.

Jackie's face lit with delight. "Of course." She smiled down at Bella Jo. "Hello, sweetheart."

"I want to make a phone call before I start supper."

Jackie nodded, cooing to baby Bella. Fawn paused to watch Bella grin around the milky nipple of the bottle. This was a new trick for the four-month-old, one she employed often with great success.

Slipping down the central hall to the bedroom that Jackie had pointed out to her, Fawn pulled her cell phone from the hip pocket of her jeans. Little remodeling had been done in here. The yellowed walls hadn't seen a fresh coat of paint in years, and the hardwood floor badly needed polishing, not to mention a throw rug. At least the twin-size bed, which boasted neither head-nor footboard, had sheets on it. The room could have used a bedside lamp. And a table to set it on.

Fawn dropped down onto the bed and punched in the familiar numbers. Within moments her grandmother answered the phone.

"*Auweni*?"

"It's Fawn, Grandmother."

"*Mamalis*!" Grandmother exclaimed, using Fawn's Lenape name. "I am happy to hear from you. I have prayed to Jesus for your safe trip. How is Jackie?"

"She is tired and weak, Grandmother, and her son is not what I expected. Your prayers are appreciated."

"He is *kikape*?"

"Yes, he is single," Fawn confirmed. It had

been one of their fears. Unattached men did not respond well to illness. Or infants. Or anything that hampered their freedom. A married man who had given up his freedom willingly would have been more inclined to open his heart and home. He would also have had help.

"But that's not the problem," she continued. "Things are worse between him and his mother than I realized. He's very resentful."

"I remember two girls with much resentment toward a parent."

"A drunkard who kills himself and your mother is a little different from a woman who deadens her pain with drugs," Fawn pointed out.

"Is it?" Grandmother asked. "Seems to me the only real difference is an accidental house fire."

Fawn bit her lip. "Perhaps you're right."

"My daughter's husband was a habitual drunk," Grandmother said calmly, "but he meant no harm, *Mamalis*."

"He meant no harm," Fawn pointed out

softly, "but they are both dead. Besides, it's been years since Jackie used illicit drugs."

"But does her son know this?"

"I'm not sure," Fawn admitted. "Apparently, they've been estranged for a long time."

"Patience," Grandmother counseled. "Patience—"

"And prayer," Fawn said for her, smiling. It was Grandmother's prescription for every situation.

Her *kmis*, or elder sister, was not so sanguine. Though older by only sixteen minutes, Dawn took her position as *kmis* very seriously. Those slim sixteen minutes might as well have been sixteen years, given how protective Dawn could be with her twin. She had not been in favor of Fawn undertaking this mission before Christmas.

Both Fawn and Grandmother had argued that putting it off until after the first of the year would be unwise, given the precarious state of Jackie's health. They thought it best to settle the matter and hopefully give Jackie a peaceful, happy Christmas, especially considering that it could be her last.

Dawn got on the phone as soon as Grandmother and Fawn ended their conversation. Obviously she'd been near their grandmother, listening in on every word.

"You knew Dixon Lyons could be single," Dawn pointed out, skipping right over the greeting, "so what's the real problem?"

Fawn mentally sighed. "Like I told Grandmother, he's more resentful than I expected."

"No. I don't buy it. You were prepared to deal with a single man. There's something more." Fawn could almost feel the thoughts churning in her twin's mind. "He's hunky, isn't he?"

Fawn plopped back onto the bed. "He's gorgeous," she admitted. "But he can see that Jackie is ill, and it makes no difference to him."

"Bring Bella and Jackie and come home," Dawn ordered. "We'll be her family. We—"

"*Petapan*," Fawn interrupted, using Dawn's

Lenape name. "We should at least give him a chance to do the right thing, don't you think?"

After a long silence, Dawn said softly, "Whatever happens, remember our mother." Then she ended the call.

As if I could forget, Fawn thought. *As if a daughter could ever forget her mother's mistakes.*

Chapter Two

How dare she? Dixon fumed, letting the wind suck the door closed behind him. Pretty little Fawn Whoever obviously didn't know his mother very well or she wouldn't have lectured him like that.

Giving birth to you ought to be enough.

He mimicked the words in his head as he skirted between the front end of the pickup and the storage room at the end of the carport.

What did this Fawn person know about it? She'd never seen his mother sleep around the clock after one of her benders or heard the whispers at the grocery store. Fawn had never watched some strange man literally drop her loopy mother in the front yard and drive away while she reeled toward the house. He'd always wondered what was so wrong with him that she couldn't stay home and sober—until he'd realized that his grandmother was right. What was so wrong was *Jackie*.

So why was she here now? After all those years when all he'd wanted was for her to come home and settle down, now all he wanted was for her to go away before she ruined everything good in his life. He finally had a healthy relationship with his dad, worked for the family business, a plan for the future, a *family*, and that hadn't been easy, given the animosity toward his father from his maternal grandparents, who had raised Dixon.

His grandparents and his dad had tiptoed around each other for years after Gregory Lyons had returned to town following an eight-year stint in the army. At twelve, Dixon had barely even remembered his father, despite many letters and photographs and a few visits. Greg had a new family by then, a wife, Lucinda, and a baby son. Jackie had gone into a tailspin upon Greg's return, partying for days at a time. Dixon's grandparents had feared that Greg would sue for custody, so they'd kept him at arm's length. Greg and Lucinda had soon enlarged their family with a second son, but Dixon's time with his dad and his dad's family had remained limited until Grandma Crane died in a fall when Dixon was twelve.

With Jackie spending more time partying than with her son, Grandpa could no longer find excuses to keep Dixon away from his Lyons family, who had proved remarkably accepting of him. They'd even asked him to live with them, but he couldn't leave his grandfather alone with Jackie, and that had caused some awkwardness on all sides until he'd turned sixteen and could drive himself over to his dad's place whenever he'd wanted. He'd really gotten to know his brothers then, and he'd started to learn his dad's trade, building. Dixon had turned out to be a more than fair carpenter.

Jackie had barely waited for Dixon to turn eighteen before she'd taken off with Harry Griffin. After his grandfather's death a couple years later, Dixon worked for his dad, and they'd done well together.

Dixon had been surprised when Jackie had actually married Harry. Loud, stout and bald as a pool cue, Harry had stood a good head shorter than Jackie. Assuming that his mother was just using the affable trucker to get her teeth fixed, because her drug use had destroyed her once beautiful smile, Dixon had expected her to return to War Bonnet after she'd gotten what she'd needed from the man, but she'd claimed to be happy and had always described Harry as a "fine man." Dixon had always privately supposed that Harry either had money or was more indulgent of Jackie's partying ways than her parents had been.

From the looks of her, she hadn't mended her ways over the years. She looked closer to sixty-four than forty-four. And he really did not need her reappearing after all these years with some unmarried mommy and baby in tow. No matter how stunningly beautiful that little mother might be.

A brisk wind rattled dead leaves across the crisp brown grass surrounding the house. Dixon turned up his collar and hunched his shoulders to protect his ears as he descended the gentle slope that led him the fifty yards or so to the barn, deliberately turning his attention to the waiting livestock and away from his unwanted guests.

The red sheet metal structure loomed dark and large in the cold, windy night. Newly oiled, the door hinges merely whispered as he pushed the narrow panel inward and stepped over the sill. Three horses and the restless heifer snuffled and shifted in the loamy blackness. The body heat of the live-stock warmed this corner considerably, but if the outdoor temperature dropped much further, the heaters he'd installed last year would cycle on.

Reaching up, he switched on an overhead light and swung it to illuminate the nearest stall, where the heifer awaited his attention. He'd haltered and hobbled her, as the local veterinarian, Stark Burns, had suggested, to keep her from opening the stitches that ran from the dew claw to midhock of her left hind leg. She was not a happy patient. Using the pill pusher, he got the medication down her then unwrapped the leg, applied the prescribed salve and put on a new bandage, while avoiding the vicious swipe of an angry tail.

The wound was still fresh, and he couldn't see any improvement yet. Worse, the heifer appeared to be losing weight. That could be disastrous for a pregnant cow. Dixon tipped extra feed into her trough and mixed a few sugar cubes into it to tempt her before leaving her to go see to the horses.

He took care of the geldings, Jag and Phantom, first. Both were big, powerful cutting horses that he'd dearly love to show professionally. The stallion, Romeo, was meant to be his ticket to competing with the other two horses. The sleek chestnut bay had the bloodlines of cutting horse royalty, but he'd been born early and extremely small. Dixon had taken the chance that he would grow to a suitable size, and he'd been right. By spring Romeo would be old enough to start training. Then all they needed was one good showing at competition. After that, Romeo would get a chance to prove he could produce— or, more accurate, reproduce. The stud fees should allow Dixon to try his hand at cutting horse competitions without risking the ranch or his normal income. It was a long-range plan that his dad fully endorsed, and Dixon had worked patiently to bring to fruition.

As was his habit, he spent some time with the skittish stallion, gentling and grooming the animal. While he worked with his hands, his mind worked over his problems, specifically his mother. He couldn't deny that at times he felt lonely living out here on the ranch by himself, but he had plans and a purpose for his life, and he wasn't about to let

Jackie throw a wrench into all that. The Bible told him to honor his mother, and maybe Jackie had given birth to him, but she hadn't raised him, not really. His grandmother had been his real mother. He wasn't at all sure that he owed Jackie honor or anything else.

Resolved, he put away the curry brush, turned out the light and left the barn for the house. He'd tell Jackie that she and her friends could stay the night, then he'd take a shower and figure out something for dinner. Surely they could manage one difficult night without resorting to ugliness. He prayed about that as he trudged up the slope to the house.

The wind felt bitterly sharp, as if the temperature had dropped ten degrees in the hour or less he'd been in the barn. He let himself into the welcomed warmth of central heating and immediately caught the heady aroma of sizzling steak, his stomach growling. Frown in place, he stepped into the doorway of the kitchen even as he shucked his coat, his hat still on his head. Pretty Fawn stood at his stove turning a slab of chicken-fried steak in his biggest cast-iron skillet. Evidently they'd brought groceries because he certainly hadn't had that steak on hand. Before he could comment, he heard Jackie playfully say, "Boo!"

A quick glance showed her playing peek-aboo with the baby, who sat in a carrier on top of the table, waving her arms excitedly while Jackie draped a soft blanket over her little face and quickly pulled it away.

"I see you, Bella Jo. Peekaboo!"

Instantly, Dixon flashed back to an early memory, one he had almost forgotten.

He crouched behind his grandmother's easy chair, quiet as a mouse. Suddenly his mom popped over the top, reaching down to tickle him.

"Boo! I found you, Dixon Lee. Mama always finds her boy."

She scrambled around to sit on the floor with him, hugging and tickling. They were both laughing when his grandmother came in to say that she was going into town.

"Wait a minute. We'll go with you," Jackie said eagerly.

Grandma made a face and shook her head. "No, Jackie. It'll take too long, and it's way too much trouble for a quick trip to the store."

"But I haven't been out of the house in days except to work."

"Well, whose fault is that? You should've thought of the consequences of your actions a long time ago."

Setting him aside, Jackie stiffly rose. "I made a mistake, and I'm never going to stop paying for it, am I?" she choked out.

His grandmother looked at him then, and Dixon thought, Me. I'm the mistake. *His grandmother rolled her eyes, then turned and left the room. A moment later his mother also left the room, slamming the door angrily behind her and calling for his grandfather.*

How long had it been before he had seen her again? It had seemed like weeks, but he knew it had probably only been days. To a boy of three, days might as well have been weeks, though. The old bitterness welled up in him.

"You can't stay," he announced baldly, the words out before he even thought them. Jackie looked up, surprise and dismay on her lined face before she carefully masked her emotions. He lifted off his hat, steeling himself, and plunked it onto the hook beside the door before tossing aside his coat and actually moving into the other room. "You are not going to ruin my Christmas," he said, trying to sound reasonable, "and we both know that's what will happen if you stay."

"I've never wanted to ruin anything for you, Dixon," his mother said softly, sitting back in her chair, "but we have nowhere else to go."

We? Dixon shook his head. So, it was a package deal. He turned his attention to Fawn. Did Jackie think dragging along this young beauty and her kid would soften him, make him more apt to open his home? What an opinion she must have of him, of men in general.

"And where's your husband in all this?" he demanded of the dark-haired beauty. If they were asking him to take them in, he had a right to know. Didn't he?

She looked stunned, standing there with a plate of chicken-fried steaks piled one on top of another, her dark, tip-tilted eyes wide. "I beg your pardon?"

"Your husband," Dixon repeated. "Why isn't he taking care of y'all?"

Blinking, she shook her head. "I'm not married."

No, of course she wasn't. Why was he not surprised? He slid his mother a disgusted look and stomped out of the room.

Going straight to his bedroom, he made short work of getting clean and dressed again. He was not—*not*—in any way pleased or relieved or even curious about how or why the woman cooking in his kitchen could show up with a baby and no husband. This itchy, nervous, supersensitive feeling was nothing more than concern.

He wondered what to do with himself, only

to determine that this was *his* house and he'd be hung before he'd be relegated to his bedroom by a pair of unwelcome interlopers and an infant.

After stomping on his boots, he headed back to the kitchen, but at the last moment he derailed into the vacant living room, where he plopped down onto the sofa and prayed for…something. Strength, wisdom, the right words. Kindness? He didn't know what to ask for. He just knew that he needed help.

"You're crying."

Fawn hadn't seen Jackie cry since Harry had died, and God knew she'd had plenty of reasons to weep. She'd been strong for so long now, but her weakened physical state was obviously wearing on her.

"I knew he'd be bitter," Jackie whispered raggedly, "but…" Shaking her head, she wiped at her eyes and focused on the baby. "It'll be okay." She managed a wobbly smile. "Despite everything, this has always been my home. It'll be okay."

Fawn didn't know if Jackie was trying to convince herself, comforting the baby or sending up a prayer of faith. Turning back to the stove, Fawn took a plate from the counter and filled it. She carried it to the table for Jackie then poured a glass of water and laid a knife and fork next to it, along with a paper napkin.

"Do you need me to cut the steak?"

"I'm not that far gone."

Smiling grimly, Fawn went back to the stove and filled another plate, this time with full portions. She poured iced tea into a tall tumbler, pocketed napkins, laid the knife and fork onto the plate and carried everything from the room in search of Dixon Lyons. Thankfully, she found him in the living room, sitting on the couch with his head in his hands. He had showered and changed, but even with his head bowed she could tell that he hadn't shaved. She was glad because she had the feeling that he would be wildly attractive clean-shaven, and she didn't need that distraction.

"I brought your dinner."

He jerked, as if he hadn't heard her approach. For an instant he glared up at her, but then his gaze softened and he reached for the plate, nodding.

"Thanks."

Parking the heavy stoneware plate on his thighs, he picked up the knife and fork and began to eat. When the steak cut easily, he lifted an eyebrow. He hummed when he began to chew but otherwise said nothing.

Fawn passed him the napkins and sat crosslegged on the floor in front of him. He shot her a glance but continued eating without comment. While he ate, she took the time to pray, asking for the words to make him understand the situation and face his responsibilities. When she was done, she decided that bluntness would suit this man best. Taking a deep breath, she said, "Your stepfather is dead, and your mother is dying."

Dixon dropped his fork and looked up at that. "What did you say?"

Fawn met his gaze squarely and said as

kindly as she could, "Jackie is dying. It's her heart. They've recommended her for transplant, but for many reasons she's low on the list, so it's not likely she'll live long enough to receive a new heart."

After placing his knife on the plate, Dixon carefully set the plate aside. "You're telling me that my mother's heart is so bad she's literally dying."

"Yes. And because Harry was an independent trucker, what insurance they had barely covered his debts. He left her destitute. She tried to work after his death, but her pregnancy wouldn't allow her to continue, so—"

"Whoa." Dixon held up a hand, palm out, gray eyes wide. "Pregnancy? *Her* pregnancy?"

"Of course. Apparently, she already had heart damage, but no one realized it. She was tired all the time, sick and weak a lot, headaches, nausea, various pains and swelling… They were seriously talking about ovarian cancer. When they first found out she was pregnant, we thought that explained it all. We didn't know until after Harry died that her heart was bad. And the pregnancy just wrecked it."

Dixon stared at her as if she'd spoken in a foreign language. "You're saying my mother was *pregnant* when Harry died?"

"Obviously."

"How is that obvious?" he demanded, spreading his hands.

Shrugging, Fawn braced her hands on her knees. "I'd think that *Bella* makes it obvious."

"Bella! *Bella?*"

It hit her then with the force of a slap that he really didn't know, hadn't put it together at all. Her head jerked to the side as the implications registered. "Oh, how stupid I am." No wonder he'd asked about her husband! What he must think! Shaking her head, she tried to set it all straight. "The baby is your *sister.*"

If his eyebrows had risen any higher, they'd have disappeared into his hairline. "What?"

"Bella Jo is your sister."

"But…" He couldn't seem to form words for several seconds. "Her hair…"

"Is dark like Harry's," Fawn supplied. "Or

like Harry's was before he started going bald and shaving his head."

Still, Dixon stared blankly at her. "I don't understand."

Fawn went to her knees, reaching for his right hand. She gripped it tightly with hers. It was a strong hand, long-fingered and square-palmed, calloused with much use.

"Dixon," she said carefully, "Bella is your mother and Harry's daughter."

His gray eyes plumbed hers. "Not yours?"

"No."

He gripped her so hard that Fawn feared bruises, but she showed no response.

"My sister." Suddenly, he dropped Fawn's hand and bowed his head, pressing his temples with his fingertips. "My sister."

"Yes. Born the last day of July."

He looked up again, obviously doing the mental math. "She's barely four months old."

"That's right."

"My mother's forty-four! How did this happen?"

Fawn sat back on her heels, trying to find

a suitable reply to that. "The usual way, I imagine. I know it took them both by surprise, but they were happy about it, ecstatic. Especially Harry. He was only forty, you know."

Dixon looked at her then as if she'd suddenly grown an extra nose. Lifting his hands to his head again, he fell back against the couch. "Oh. My. Word."

Fawn thought about trying to point out the ramifications in light of his mother's health issues, but he was obviously struggling with these fresh realizations, so she kept quiet. After a moment, confident that he finally understood what had brought them here and why they could not simply leave again, she quietly rose to her feet, picked up his plate and left him alone with his thoughts.

Chapter Three

His sister!

A four-month-old sister. Bella. Bella *Jo*.

Dixon could barely believe it, but evidently it was true. At forty-four, Jackie had given birth to her second child. His sister. In addition, Jackie was in ill health, but *dying*? He had much more difficulty believing that than everything else. He set it aside for the moment.

He hadn't known Harry Griffin at all, but apparently Jackie had been happily married to the man, who turned out to have been a few years her junior. Dixon recalled the times his mother had urged him to get to know his stepfather, and now he regretted that he hadn't found a way to do that, but he simply hadn't seen any reason to do it. Until now. Now that it was too late.

Unsure what to say, think or do, Dixon found himself in prayer for the third time since he'd arrived home that evening. The only words his whirling mind could come up with were, *Lord, help. I could really use some help.*

One thing about being Jackie Jo Crane Lyons Griffin's son, though, was that a fellow learned to stand up and take life like a man early on. It was either that or cower in shame. Dixon didn't cower any better than his mother did, so after a few minutes he got up, squared his shoulders and walked back into the kitchen.

His mother still sat at the table, cradling Bella Jo in her arms. Jackie pulled the nipple of a bottle from the baby's cupid's-bow mouth and tilted Bella up onto her shoulder. She'd barely landed the first pat before the baby belched like a twelve-year-old boy trying to impress his buddies.

"Always the lady," Jackie quipped, lowering Bella to her lap. "Just like your mother. Poor thing."

Dixon couldn't help a sudden fascination with the infant and went to look over his mother's shoulder. "Can't believe I have a sister."

"I don't know why not," Jackie said brightly, holding up the baby for him to view. "She looks just like you."

Dixon narrowed his eyes at the plump-faced infant. "No, she doesn't."

"She does," Jackie insisted. "Except for the dark hair, she looks just like your baby pictures."

"And your baby pictures look just like your mother's baby pictures," Fawn put in from the sink, which was full of suds.

"I have a dishwasher, you know," he pointed out, aware that he sounded surly but unable to help himself.

She shot back with, "It's full."

Surprised, he lifted an eyebrow. It took him days to fill up the dishwasher. Looking back to his mother, he asked, "Is that true? Are my baby pictures that much like yours?"

"Why do you think your father tried to name you after me?"

Now *that* was a surprise. "Dad wanted to name me Jack?"

She nodded. "We settled on my mother's maiden name and his middle name. I think he did it partly to curry favor with her. If I'd been a boy, she'd have named me Dixon. So, Greg decided you would be my mom's Dixon. Didn't matter. She still hated him."

"*Hate* is a strong word," Dixon muttered, but it wasn't far off the mark. His grandmother had been the driving force keeping him from his father. She'd always said it was to protect him, but Dixon could never figure out what she'd been trying to protect him *from*. Greg was a solid citizen, never missed a child support payment, attended church regularly, kept his nose clean and ran a successful business. Yes, he'd gotten her daughter pregnant too young, but he'd married her and tried to be a good parent, which was more than could be said for his mother.

Jackie lifted Bella onto the edge of the table, holding her there in a sitting position. "Would you put her into her carrier, son? She'll need a dry diaper soon. Then she'll go down for several hours."

"I haven't handled many babies," Dixon hedged, wiping his palms on his jeans.

"Just pick her up under her arms and lay her in the carrier," Jackie said with a chuckle. "She holds her head up well now."

Dixon wiped his hands once more then placed them just above his mother's. He lifted gently and was shocked by how little the baby weighed. "She's light as a feather!"

"Duh. She's a baby."

"What does she weigh?" he asked, gingerly laying the infant in her padded carrier seat.

"A little over fourteen pounds."

"That's all?"

"Well, she only weighed five pounds when she was born."

"Was she early?"

"About three weeks."

"But she's healthy," Fawn said.

"Perfectly healthy," Jackie confirmed, smiling.

Bella kicked a foot, and Jackie pretended to gobble her toes, which made the baby smile, her eyebrows dancing.

"She'll be laughing before long," Fawn predicted.

"Remember when I used to do that with you?" Jackie asked Dixon. "You used to howl with laughter."

"I remember you called me your mistake," Dixon blurted, quite without meaning to.

Jackie's face registered shock, and she twisted around in her chair. "I did no such thing."

"You did," he insisted quietly. "Well, as good as."

"I don't know what you heard," Jackie insisted, "but I never would have said that."

He told her then exactly what he remembered, and she shook her head sadly. "Son,

son. *You* weren't the mistake. Yes, I got pregnant and married too young, and it was much more difficult than I thought it was going to be, just as my parents predicted, but that wasn't the mistake. My real mistake was divorcing your father."

"But...you hated Dad as much as Grandma did!"

"No. No, no." Jackie shook her head, smiling sadly. "I was heartbroken when Greg came home married to Lucinda. Frankly, Dix, until Harry, I never thought I'd love again."

"I...I don't understand any of this."

She sighed. "Pride and pain make us do foolish things, Dix. I have no pride left, and Harry took care of the pain. He was a good Christian man. He forgave all my mistakes, loved me in spite of them and made me happy, even though I didn't have you with me." She looked at Bella, smiling. "We never expected to have a child of our own. He thought he couldn't. Imagine our joy last Christmas when the doctors told us we were expecting."

"I confess I'm surprised," Dixon said, looking at his now drowsy-eyed baby sister. "I wouldn't have thought you even wanted more children."

Jackie looked up, obviously surprised. "Why would you think that?"

"It's not like you were around a lot," Dixon pointed out. He didn't say that some folks would have called her neglectful. His grandmother had.

"I needed to work to help pay the bills, Dixon, and that meant either driving long distances on a daily basis or moving you away from your grandparents, which was exactly what your father wanted me to do. That was our main problem, actually. Eventually he gave me an ultimatum. And I made the wrong choice. He left, and I stayed here with you, which meant that I had to work even more, and that just made your grandmother even more critical. Eventually she was raising you, and I was…inconvenient."

Dixon hadn't realized that she'd felt that way, but he could see now how she might have. His grandmother had been a strong-willed woman of firm opinions. He didn't doubt that she'd loved him, but her love had been a rather possessive sort.

"How is Greg?" Jackie asked lightly, too lightly, interrupting Dixon's thoughts.

"Fine," Dixon answered in the same vein.

"Still married?"

"Yep."

"That's good."

Something about the way she said that set off alarm bells in Dixon's mind, which made him say, "Lucinda and the boys are fine, too."

Jackie smiled knowingly. "Your brothers must be all grown up."

"Sixteen and fourteen."

"That's quite a group of siblings," Jackie mused. "Twenty-eight, sixteen, fourteen, and four months."

"Almost twenty-nine," Dixon corrected. "I'll be twenty-nine this month."

Jackie beamed. "Yes. My two Christmas gifts. I found out about your sister on the nineteenth, the day before your twenty-eighth birthday." She laughed. "I thought they were going to tell me I had cancer. They told me I was pregnant!"

"Why didn't you tell me?" he asked, sincerely puzzled.

She sighed. "I guess I was afraid you'd say what everyone else did, that having her was foolish. Harry and I were going to bring her together to meet you as soon as she was born and able to travel, but then…" She bowed her head. "God had other plans." She looked up once more and said, "You do think I was foolish to have her, don't you?"

"I didn't say that."

"Greg would probably agree with you."

"I didn't say that," Dixon repeated more firmly.

"Your grandparents would certainly agree." She chuckled sourly. "That would probably be the first time Greg and your grandparents agreed on anything."

"No one has said you were foolish to have Bella," Dixon told her.

"Well, I don't care," she went on as if he hadn't even spoken, her fingertips brushing over Bella's tiny foot. Dixon realized that the baby had dropped off to sleep while they were talking. "She's worth it. You're both worth it."

Feeling eerily as if his mother had somehow slipped away, Dixon murmured that he was going up to the attic for some things they might need. Tossing aside a dish towel, Fawn asked if she could help. He wanted to wave her away, but he doubted he could move down the necessary items alone.

Nodding, he led the way to the game room and pulled down the hinged attic ladder. It was the one feature from the garage that he had elected to leave in place. After climbing the ladder, he switched on the attic light and went straight to the farthest corner. Fawn scrambled up after him. The white crib, with its yellow and green trim, stood collapsed against the wall, with the metal spring platform behind it and the mattress, wrapped in plastic, in front.

"What do you think?"

"That's good," Fawn said. "Bella can't sleep in her carrier for long."

They moved all three pieces to the hole in the floor then let each one down.

He got some rags while Fawn located an appropriate cleaner, and together they wiped down everything. As they worked, he considered what to do next. Obviously, he couldn't put his ill mother and baby sister out in the cold, but he worried that he didn't know the whole story yet, and he feared that Jackie might resent his father and vice versa.

Over the years, every time anything about his mother had come up, his dad had always quickly changed the subject. Not once had he expressed an opinion or a thought about her, though the man had to feel *something* for her. They were once married, after all, and had a child together. Dixon assumed that Greg's feelings for Jackie were mixed at best and most likely negative, given that few divorced couples thought highly of each other. Jackie, on the other hand, might well resent Greg and Lucinda's successful marriage and family, which could lead to some truly appalling episodes.

The best course at present seemed simply to say nothing to his father about his mother's presence. After Christmas—if Jackie stayed around that long, because Dixon had his doubts on that score—he would decide what to tell his father. They saw each other almost every day at work so it wasn't like Greg dropped by the ranch very often. Dixon reasoned that he'd surely know more about the situation by Christmas and know better what was what. He accepted that she was ill, even seriously ill, but she couldn't be actively *dying*. Could she?

Meanwhile, there was a baby in the house, and someone had to make sure that she had everything she needed. That included the best possible care. If it just so happened that care came in the best-looking package he'd ever seen, who was he to complain?

"If Jackie's as ill as you say, should Bella be in Jackie's room?" Dixon asked.

"Jackie's her mother," Fawn replied simply, "and we have a baby monitor, so whenever Bella wakes, I hear her."

That made sense, especially if Fawn slept in Dixon's old room, which he had vacated long ago. First, he'd moved to his mother's old room. Then, after his grandfather's death, he'd remodeled the master suite and moved in there.

He and Fawn carried the crib into the front bedroom, the one nearest the living room. Jackie used to complain about the noise, but since he'd moved the television into the game room, it should be quieter. Now, with a baby in the house, he was glad of that.

When he went back through the living room into the game room for the metal bedspring, Fawn followed and took up the mattress, which weighed next to nothing. They carried both back to the bedroom. Then Dixon ran to the storage room behind the carport for tools. He was bolting the metal spring platform into the center of the crib frame when he asked Fawn why she was doing all this.

"She's my friend," Fawn answered simply, tearing the protective plastic from the mattress. "My coworker. What was I supposed to do when her husband died and she fell so very ill?"

"What about your job?"

Fawn shrugged. "I can always find another job waiting tables."

"That's what you do, wait tables?"

"That's what I do right now."

"How do you plan to manage in the meantime?"

"I have a little income from my late parents' estate, and my sister and grandmother will help as needed. That's where Jackie and Bella have been until now, with us at my grandmother's."

Dixon stopped what he was doing. "I didn't know."

"She didn't want you to know until Bella was born."

Did she really think he'd have tried to talk her out of having the baby? She didn't know her own son very well. He shook his head and went back to work. "Can you hold up that corner over there?"

Fawn did as asked, keeping the platform level until he had the other three corners securely bolted in place. He set the fourth bolt and tightened everything down then took out his pliers.

"There's some sag in the middle, but I think I can tighten it up. How's that mattress?"

"Seems fine."

"Doubt we can find any crib sheets."

"I can make a twin work."

"Those are in my old room."

"I'll find them." She nodded toward the dresser, adding, "I suppose we should move that down and set the crib in the corner."

"Seems right. You get the sheet. I'll move everything."

She didn't argue, just went out to do as he'd directed. He couldn't help watching her. She moved with more grace and ease than any woman he knew. And he was mooning over her like a twelve-year-old.

Irritated with himself, he removed a few drawers, then picked up a suitcase and set it on the bed before sliding the dresser down the wall. As he was putting back the drawers, he accidentally knocked the suitcase off the bed. The top of the hard case popped open, and several items spilled out. One was a small, thick photo album. He put everything back inside and placed the suitcase back on the bed, but then he picked up the photo album and opened it.

The very first picture was that of a tiny, scrunched-up infant tucked into a large Christmas stocking. That had to be him. The next page was a more formal photo, labeled, "Six Mos." He wore a tiny suit of baby blue with short pants and satin shoes. The page opposite was a picture of Bella Jo, looking like a doll in frilly pink. He saw it then, the family resemblance, though she had more hair and looked smaller, younger. His sister.

His grandmother had been quick to point out that Bass and Phillip were his half brothers, but he wondered if she would feel the same about Bella. He hoped she wouldn't, but he didn't know. He loved Bass and Phil. He supposed he would love Bella, too. She was a sweet little thing. He wondered who she'd take more after, Jackie or Harry.

He hoped it was Harry. Then he wondered what Fawn would think of that. And just the fact that he might care about her opinion made him wish that he'd never laid eyes on the dark-haired beauty.

Chapter Four

Nothing more was said about their leaving. Or staying. Fawn thought about pressing Dixon for clarification on the matter, but after he set up the crib, he made himself scarce for the rest of the evening. Exhausted, Jackie followed the baby to bed shortly after 8:00 p.m., but Fawn watched television until Bella woke at ten for a bottle. As usual, the baby woke again about five in the morning and went right back to sleep after her bottle, but Fawn always found sleep elusive after that early-morning feeding. After making coffee, she sat down at the kitchen table with her Bible and daily devotional.

She had just finished reading when Dixon walked in. Freshly shaved, he looked younger and strikingly handsome. He went straight to the coffeepot and took down an insulated travel mug from the cabinet above it.

"You're up early."

"Your sister likes breakfast early."

"Let me guess who fixed the bottle."

"Bella can't fix her own."

He filled the mug and screwed the top onto it before turning to face her, leaning his hip against the counter. "My mother is so unwell she can't manage a bottle of formula?"

"Yes."

He nodded and sipped his coffee, his gaze carefully averted. Then he broke off a banana from a bunch on the counter and began to peel and eat it.

"I'll gladly make your breakfast," she offered, starting to rise from her chair.

Waving her back down, he shook his head. "No time." He went to the refrigerator, took a packaged sandwich out of a box in the freezer and carried it to the microwave.

A minute later he tossed the banana peel, plucked the sandwich from the microwave oven and grabbed his travel mug. "Gotta go."

"You work on Saturday?"

"Yep."

"Uh, Dixon, I was wondering…"

He paused in the doorway to the mudroom. "Yeah?"

"A Christmas tree for the house would be fun and really cheer up Jackie."

Shrugging, he turned. "We usually just cut a red cedar. I've tried to eradicate them on the range, but there are a few around the house. I really don't have time for cutting one right now, though."

"Do you have ornaments?"

"Sure. Up in the attic."

"Okay. Now, about the fireplace. Jackie loves a fire. Would you mind if I brought in some wood and—"

"Yeah," he interrupted, "I do. Since it's a propane fireplace. Just flip the switch on the side of the mantel."

"Ah."

"Now, I gotta go." He turned away.

"One more thing."

Sighing, he turned back. "Make it quick. I have to doctor an injured cow before I can get to work."

"How can I reach you? In case of an emergency."

For a moment he merely glared, but then he barked out ten digits. She whipped out her phone and quickly tapped them in, repeating them aloud. A second later his phone started to ring.

"Now you have my number, too."

Nodding, he turned and walked into the mudroom, the phone in his hip pocket still ringing. After a moment she tapped the icon that ended the call. She heard him pulling on his outerwear and mere seconds later he left the house. She returned to her chair and sat down to think, then called her sister. Dawn didn't have any more experience with men than Fawn did, but Grandmother was already at work, and Dawn was far more careful and suspicious of the opposite gender than Fawn.

Surely between them they could safely discern Dixon's likely reactions if Fawn did what she was contemplating.

Dawn answered groggily. "I'm the sister who sleeps in. Remember?"

"Your alarm goes off in five minutes."

"Then this had better be a five-minute-long conversation."

Chuckling, Fawn told her twin what Dixon had said about the Christmas tree. Dawn agreed that he, conveniently, hadn't told Fawn that she *couldn't* cut down a tree herself and likely wouldn't be upset if she spared him the effort.

"Send me a pic when you get it decorated."

Fawn promised, but privately she was more concerned about pleasing Dixon Lyons. She told herself that it was because he hadn't committed to taking care of Jackie and Bella yet, but she feared that the reason was more personal, and that frightened her. Was she more her mother's daughter than she knew? Even when he was being contrary, she liked Dixon. Was she ignoring the warning signs, as her mother must have done with her father? When Dawn's alarm went off, Fawn felt a sense of relief. If her overprotective sister ever suspected how strongly Fawn was attracted to Dixon, she'd be on the road to War Bonnet within the hour to judge him and the situation for herself.

After changing, feeding, bathing and dressing the baby, then getting her down for her nap and making Jackie comfortable, Fawn found it was late morning before she was able to go out in search of the tree. Thankfully, Dixon didn't seem to lock anything, and she found the tools she needed, along with a wheelbarrow in the little shed built into the end of the carport. The task was more laborious than she'd imagined, and to make matters worse, the tree fell on her. It wasn't large enough to do any damage, but cedar needles proved surprisingly sticky and itchy.

Lunch had to be handled and the baby and Jackie seen to again before Fawn could decorate. Desperate for a shower, she worked quickly, getting the tree into the stand in front of the living room window, stringing the multicolored lights, hanging the ornaments and threading wide, wired, red ribbon through the branches. Finding no angel for the top, she used a tinsel star that had seen better days. All in all, she thought it turned out well. Sitting in front of a cheery fire, Jackie seemed to agree.

"That really takes me back. So much has changed around here, but that really takes me back."

Fawn snapped a picture with her phone and texted it to her sister, then rushed off to shower and change her sticky, itchy clothes just in time to start dinner.

Dixon came in as she was getting the bread ready for the oven. "That smells good."

"Homemade chicken noodle soup and my grandmother's biscuits. They'll take about twenty minutes if you want to shower first."

"That'll work. Took care of that stubborn old heifer on my way in."

"What's wrong with the heifer?"

"Nasty cut on her rear leg. It's been stitched, but it doesn't look good."

"I can ask my grandmother what she recommends."

"Your grandmother's a vet?"

"No, a nurse, but she has a healing way with all living things."

"Huh."

She'd seen that skeptical look before, but she made no comment. Neither did he, not then and not after he walked into the living room and pointedly looked at the Christmas tree. In fact, he must've noticed it when he'd driven in. The lights would undoubtedly show through the front window, but he simply walked past the fireplace and into the hallway without a single word.

When tears of disappointment sprang to her eyes, Fawn felt like kicking herself. Or him.

Dixon told himself that it was foolish to feel disappointed that she hadn't waited for him to cut down the tree and help decorate it. The last couple years he hadn't even bothered with a tree because he lived alone and knew he'd be spending the holiday with his dad and the rest of the family. Still, he'd felt an unexpected warmth when he'd spied the glowing lights of the Christmas tree in the front window. It was nice not to come home to a cold, dark house, even if what awaited him inside was a lot of problems. If it had only been Fawn waiting for him... But he dared not think like that.

Then memories had assailed him as he'd taken in the tree, years past when he and his mother and grandparents had made a whole evening out of putting up the Christmas tree. He'd suddenly longed for what had never truly been, wondering why it was so easy to forget the good times and so difficult to forget the bad.

He had suddenly wished that they had never come; yet the idea that decorating this tree tonight with Jackie and Fawn would have banished bad memories had washed over him. He felt robbed, especially if Jackie was dying, as Fawn insisted. He turned off the thought.

Like his dad said, worry didn't add a single day to anyone's life. Prayer, on the other hand...

Lord, if it's true that she's as sick as Fawn says, have mercy on her.

He left it at that and swiftly cleaned up. When he returned to the kitchen, it was to find Fawn carrying food into the formal dining area. He'd removed the wall between the old formal dining room and the living room to make it one large open space with cased openings that gave good lines of sight from the kitchen into both areas. The Christmas tree, however, stood in the central window, the one space that would be difficult to see from the breakfast nook where he normally took his meals, so Jackie requested that the meal be served in the dining room.

Dixon had no quarrel with the arrangement. With the fire blazing and the tree twinkling, he felt the first real stirrings of Christmas spirit. He certainly had no complaints about the food. The soup was hearty and delicious. The bread, though, was the stuff of dreams—high, airy, flaky. He'd have made a real pig of himself if Fawn hadn't said she'd make gravy with breakfast if enough biscuits were left over.

As the meal progressed, however, he felt more and more uncomfortable, so he escaped to his room and watched a movie on the TV there. All the while, he wondered what Fawn and Jackie were doing, but when he slipped out after the movie, all was quiet and dark, so he turned in for the night.

He tried very hard not to be too impressed when he walked into the kitchen the next morning to find a skillet of thick, fragrant sausage gravy steaming on the stove and a plate of warmed biscuits waiting for him. As it was Sunday, he came in dressed in his darkest jeans, white shirt, blue tie and his best sport coat.

Fawn wore her usual boots, jeans and loose top, this one plaid with a collar and cuffs. She'd braided her hair and left it swinging in one long plait between her shoulder blades, slender tendrils twining with the chunky turquoise orbs dangling from her dainty earlobes. He didn't know how she managed to look so stunning with such casual ease. She seemed as kind as she was beautiful, too. How many people would do what she was doing for Jackie and his sister? He realized suddenly that he would very much like to be her friend.

For a moment he thought about inviting her to attend church with him, but then he'd have to ask Jackie, too, and take along Bella, all of which would require some explanation. Given that he had yet to mention any of them to his dad's family, he couldn't very well just appear in public with them. So he said nothing, just thanked her for the breakfast as he rose from his chair. She looked faintly startled.

"Uh. You're welcome. I'll have lunch ready by noon. BLTs and potato skins. Your mom really likes both, and she doesn't eat enough."

He really liked both, as well, and Fawn was

an excellent cook, but his stepmom almost always invited him over for Sunday dinner, so he said only, "I'll keep that in mind," as he headed for the door.

"Is it the tree?" she asked.

He paused, trying to decide what to tell her. Finally, he shook his head. "No."

"I didn't mean to upset you. Since you were so busy, I thought I'd just take care of it. I hoped it would cheer up the place, bring in a little Christmas spirit."

"Yes," he said. "It does. I didn't realize how much it would until I saw it. Then…" He shrugged. "I guess I suddenly wished I could've taken part."

"Oh." She looked down at her toes. "Well, I wasn't trying to keep you out. It just never occurred to me. It's been a while since I've been around a man much. I don't remember my grandpa, and my father died when I was eight."

"Aw, I'm sorry. What happened?"

"He was a drunk," she said flatly. "He set

the house on fire accidentally. My mother tried to pull him out. They both died."

He stared at her for several seconds, at a loss for words. Finally, he said, "That's awful." Then he felt he had to add, "I'm sorry. For everything."

She smiled tentatively. "Me, too."

Nodding, he headed for the door, guilt dogging him every step of the way. He hated the anger and resentment that he felt for his mother and the way it had splashed over onto Fawn in the beginning. He hated that he was ashamed of his own mother and that he didn't want to be seen with her or tell the rest of the family about her. He hated that strangers showed her more understanding and kindness than he could. He told himself that he couldn't have handled the situation any other way, however, and when he joined the rest of the Lyons family in their customary pew, he felt mainly relief at not having to tell them about his mother's presence or the existence of his baby sister. Still, when Lucinda invited him home with the rest of the family for Sunday dinner as usual, Dixon couldn't quite make himself agree. So he came up with an excuse.

"I better not. That old heifer of mine's not doing too good. I need to give her as much attention as I can today."

His father clapped him on the shoulder. "Let me know if you need help, son."

Dixon smiled. "Will do."

Then he took himself home, irritated by how much he anticipated Fawn's cooking. And just the sight of her. Why'd she have to be so wonderful, anyway? He kept trying to find some flaw, but not only was she lovely to look at, she was selfless, kind and caring. She had the most beautiful face he'd ever seen. Her hair couldn't have been any blacker or more lustrous, and though she stood at least a foot shorter than he did, she was perfectly proportioned, with skin that looked like caramel silk. He was finding it increasingly difficult not to touch her just to see if it was as smooth as it looked. He didn't like being so drawn to his mother's champion.

The meal did not disappoint, and with Bella awake and charming everyone with her gurgles, squeals and smiles, he couldn't help enjoying himself, which just added to the guilt he already felt.

He escaped to the barn at the earliest opportunity, only to find the cow in a very foul mood and that the wound on the heifer's leg still looked red, angry and swollen. She couldn't kick, so she tried to squash him between her body and the stall fencing while he attempted to rewrap her wound.

"I'd flatten you, too, if you kept me tied up like that."

Surprised that Fawn had followed him and managed to enter the barn without his knowledge, Dixon dropped the unrolled end of the bandage in the dirt. Irritated, he balled up the whole thing and tossed it over the rail before pushing up to his feet. She stood there in a big canvas coat, the cuffs rolled back. The coat was obviously a man's and much too large for her but looked warm. If she had gloves, she wasn't wearing them.

"Sorry about that," she said.

Dixon pointed at the cabinet fixed to the wall just inside the door.

"Bring me another bandage."

She went to the cabinet, rummaged around and found the right packet. When she returned to the stall, instead of simply handing over the bandage, she let herself inside and went to the cow's head, frowning. "She's on too short a halter."

"I'll loosen it when I'm done here."

Fawn patted the cow then sidled around it, keeping a hand on the rough black hide.

"She's pregnant."

"Yep."

"You should untie her back legs."

"It's to keep her from breaking open these stitches."

Shaking her head, Fawn said, "Too stressful and uncomfortable for her. Remove the hobble. She'll calm down."

"She'll kick me!" Dixon exclaimed before emphatically holding out his hand for the bandage.

Fawn gave him a droll look. "You're not smart enough to keep from getting kicked by a haltered cow?"

Dixon glowered, but something told him that she was right. He dropped down to his haunches and gingerly removed the hobble. With Fawn at her side, the heifer didn't so much as swish her tail, and when the hobble dropped away, the cow immediately shifted, blew and lowered her head. Fawn came and peeked at the wound before digging something out of the pocket of her coat and handing it to Dixon. It was a plastic baggie filled with a yellowish paste.

"Will you try this on the wound? Grandmother says it draws out infection and reduces swelling. It won't hurt, I promise."

Frowning doubtfully, Dixon opened the baggie and sniffed, catching hints of honey and something sharpish. He removed a tube of ointment from his own pocket and held it up. "The vet gave me this."

"So use that, too. For all the good it seems to be doing."

He uncapped the tube and squirted a line of the goo all along the wound. After replacing the cap, he returned the tube to his pocket. Wisely, Fawn passed Dixon the bandage and moved back to the cow's head without further comment. Dixon squatted there on his haunches for several heartbeats, the baggie in one hand and the bandage in the other. He looked at the jagged, inflamed line of the wound and thought, *Why not?*

Opening the corner of the baggie, he squeezed out the paste, laying it in a line alongside the prescription gel. He closed the bag and quickly ripped the paper package protecting the bandage to begin wrapping the bandage around the animal's leg.

While he worked, Fawn spoke softly to the cow, patting the animal as if it was a pet. Dixon didn't recognize any of the words she used, the language unlike any he'd heard. As swiftly as possible, he molded the self-adhering mesh around the wounded limb. To his surprise, the heifer barely moved. He glanced at the head of the stall to find Fawn feeding the cow from her hand.

"What are you giving her?"

"Crackers. Cows like them because they're salty."

"Obviously. She's not been eating. I've been trying to tempt her with sugar, but she's not been cooperating."

"She'll eat now," Fawn said, lengthening the halter rope. As he finished off the bandage, she crumbled crackers into the feedbox. When he went to add more grain, the cow already had her nose buried deep in the box, her tail swishing happily.

Dixon took the hobble and let both himself and Fawn out of the stall. "Where'd you learn about cows?"

"My grandmother has a milk cow. And chickens and rabbits. How come you don't have chickens?"

"Too much trouble. With the cattle and horses, I have my hands full."

"You have a good place for a chicken coop," she said. Then, abruptly, she asked,

"Why do you have three horses when you can only ride one?"

"The two geldings, Phantom and Jag, are cutting horses, very useful on a ranch. The stallion, Romeo, is a moneymaker, or will be once he's trained and shown."

She tilted her head, a sign, he had come to realize, that she was thinking. "Do you always name your horses after expensive automobiles?"

Dixon chuckled. She was quick. "Caught that, did you?" He moved to Romeo's stall and hung his forearms on the top rung.

"Rolls Royce Phantom, Jaguar and Alfa Romeo."

He nodded. "Yep. The point is, I'd rather have these guys than those cars."

Laughing, she said, "Clever and appropriate."

"I thought so." He cut her a curious look. "What was that you were speaking earlier? It wasn't English."

"Well, it's primarily *Unami*. Some call it *Lenape*, though that word means *man* or *people.* My mother was almost full-blood *Leni-Lenape*, what you would call Delaware Indian."

"Then you're Native American."

She smiled. "Mostly."

"No wonder you're so beautiful." She looked as shocked as he felt, the words slipping out completely unintended. "I mean, no wonder your hair and eyes are so black and your skin is so…smooth."

Her "Thank you" came out in a strangled voice, but then she quickly said, "I'd better get back to the house."

Dixon muttered, "Gonna work the horses."

She hurried away, and when he finished mentally kicking himself, he determined to do his very best to keep his distance.

He put his hand in his coat pocket and felt the half-filled baggie there.

Clearly the woman was dangerous to his good sense. If nothing else.

Chapter Five

No wonder you're so beautiful.

Those unexpected words haunted Fawn—and apparently drove Dixon away, because she saw him only at breakfast and dinner for the rest of the week. With the baby, he made faces and silly noises, perfectly pleasant, but he ignored Fawn and Jackie. He did, however, eat and eat plenty. Once, Fawn asked how the cow was doing.

"Getting along," he muttered, not even looking up.

She didn't ask again.

By Friday, the pantry and the baby were nearly bare, so Fawn did what her grandmother had taught her to do: she took stock, devised a menu, made a list, estimated the cost of every item and counted out the cash. What little disability and survivor's Social Security Jackie and Bella drew monthly was currently entrusted to Fawn's care, and she was careful not to pay her own expenses from it. The shopping list and the cash she left on the breakfast table next to Dixon's plate. When he came in to eat, he couldn't help seeing it, and he wasn't happy.

"You sure make yourself at home, don't you? Guess you think you're just going to take over around here."

Stung, she turned her back to him and began scrubbing the countertop. "Actually I think I'm going to clean the kitchen."

Jackie shuffled in a few moments later, the fussy baby in her arms. Fawn began rinsing and drying her hands.

"Someone woke up early," Dixon commented, sounding pleased.

"Rather, she slept late," Jackie corrected, yawning. "She slept through until just now."

"I have a bottle ready for her," Fawn said, coming to take the baby so Jackie could sit down. "Did you change her?"

"I did. We're running low on diapers, by the way."

Fawn said nothing to that. She could always take Bella to town with her and do the shopping, but she hated to leave Jackie alone. It had been too long since Jackie had seen a doctor, another matter Fawn needed to take up with Dixon soon. Feeding Bella took precedence, however. She picked up the waiting bottle and slipped the nipple between the baby's quivering lips.

"I think it's warmer in the living room," Jackie murmured, but before she could turn away, Fawn stopped her.

"Sit down and eat while your breakfast is still hot." She carried the baby back to Jackie and waited for the older woman to take a seat at the table before handing the infant to her. Jackie cuddled her daughter close while Fawn quickly removed Jackie's breakfast from the warming oven. She placed the food on the table and took Bella back.

"This looks good," Jackie said, picking up her spoon and casting a careful glance at her son.

"It is," Dixon confirmed, surprising Fawn with the compliment.

No wonder you're so beautiful.

Flustered and confused, given his combativeness that morning, Fawn turned away, gently rocking the baby, who finished the bottle in record time. Fawn lifted Bella to her shoulder, got the expected hearty burp and tucked the little one onto her hip while she continued wiping down the counters.

"You seem to have ample experience with infants," Dixon commented after a few minutes.

The words flowed over Fawn in a series of tiny shocks, but she neither turned nor flinched.

"I started babysitting when I was eleven. Besides, *Lenape* women are raised to multitask."

"I thought *Lenape* meant *man.*"

"Or *people*," Fawn reminded him.

"In this case, it means *the* people," Jackie put in. "The Delaware are a matriarchal society, you know. They produce very strong women."

"That explains a lot," Dixon commented drily.

Fawn could feel her blood pressure rising. She worked to tamp down her ire for several seconds before she could say, "I'm doing laundry today. Do you want me to do your laundry? Or am I not supposed to use your washer and dryer?"

Chair legs scraped on the tile floor. Not trusting herself to fully face him without completely losing her temper, she half turned, glancing over her shoulder, the baby cradled against her side. Dixon stood in front of his chair, poking the shopping list into his shirt pocket.

"Use whatever you like," he retorted, heading for the mudroom, "but I do my own laundry." The money, she saw, remained on the table. He turned in the doorway and looked at his mother. "I'll be home early."

Fawn shot a look at Jackie, who appeared to be hiding a smile behind a spoon.

"My boy growls," she said as the outside door closed behind him, "but he always does the right thing in the end."

Fawn said nothing to that. Truth required no comment, and if, in the end, Jackie's faith in her son proved false, well then Fawn would do what was necessary.

Guilt had become Dixon's constant companion. He felt guilty for resenting his mother, who was so obviously ill. He felt guilty for not telling his dad about her presence and for telling no one about his sister. Most of all, he felt guilty for enjoying so very much the benefits of having Fawn around. It irked him, in fact, that she was so easy to live with, so easy to like, so easy to talk to, not to mention easy on the eyes.

His dad maintained that not all women were as difficult to live with as his mother and grandmother, but Dixon's experience proved otherwise. Every girl he'd ever dated had been more trouble than she was worth in the end, always yapping at him about something, never saying exactly what she meant, expecting him to decipher hidden meanings in everything. He'd about decided that he was going to stay single for the rest of his life, especially given the slim pickings in the War Bonnet area.

Fawn was a quiet one, tranquil somehow even when busy. He'd rattled her this morning, but he'd had to work at it, and if he was honest, he'd enjoyed himself. To a point. He liked having her in the house. It was nice not to come home to a cold, empty building, and he'd never eaten better.

The baby was no bother, either. His mother, on the other hand, was easy to ignore. Too easy. In fact, he wasn't entirely sure who was ignoring whom. Whenever he entered a room, Jackie seemed to shortly leave it. In some ways, it was almost as if she was neglecting him all over again. As contradictory as it seemed, even as he sought to avoid her, he resented that she seemed to avoid him.

*Did you ever ask yourself why your mother
did those things?*

Fawn's words just made the situation
worse, and he spent too much time dwelling
on it. He was half-mad with it by the time his
father dropped by to check on his progress.

"How's it going?"

Greg was a handsome man who had spent
too much time in the sun, so he looked a little older than his forty-six years. His eyes
were more blue than gray and his hair a little darker than Dixon's, which made the silver stand out. He had thickened around the
middle, but the nature of his work had given
him a powerful physique. Though he stood
only an inch or so taller than Dixon's own
six feet, he felt huge.

Dixon stopped staining the interior of the
kitchen cabinets, set aside his implements
and cleaned his hands on a rag. "Getting
there. The exterior of these cabinets need a
second coat of sealant, though."

"No problem. When you're done with
the inside, give the outside a light sanding,

then spray everything with a final coat of high gloss."

Dixon made a face. "A high gloss finish on the interior wouldn't be my preference, but this should've been finished a long time ago, so I'll do it your way. It's just been one thing after another on this job. You're probably even more frustrated than I am about it."

Cuffing him lightly on the shoulder, Greg said, "Aw, we'll get it done, son. Just gives us more time to spend together."

Suddenly, Dixon couldn't take it anymore. He was done keeping secrets from his father.

"Dad, I have to tell you something. About Jackie."

Greg sobered. "What is it, Dix?"

"She's here. At my house, I mean. And she has a baby."

Greg's jaw dropped. "A *baby*?"

Dixon tossed aside the rag. "I have a sister, just over four months old." Greg clapped a hand over his mouth. "I know," Dixon said. "Just when you think Jackie's done it all, she comes up with a new one."

Greg blinked, shrugged, shook his head. "I don't know what to say."

"There's more. Jackie's sick. I mean, seriously ill. Her heart, apparently." Greg gasped. "And my stepfather is dead, killed in an accident on the highway."

"Oh, Dixon." Greg shook his head sorrowfully. "What are you going to do?"

Dixon ran both hands through his hair. "I don't know. You remember what she was like before she married Harry. But there's Bella Jo now, and Jackie's…sick." He couldn't bring himself to say *dying*.

"How bad is she?" Greg asked, his face craggy with concern.

Dixon frowned. "Doesn't look too good to me."

Sighing deeply, Greg asked, "What about the baby?"

"Bella's fine. She's a cutie, dark hair and eyes. They say she looks like me."

Greg smiled wanly. "Jackie must be happy about that. She always imagined a little girl who could wear her baby things." His face clouded then. "Your grandmother got rid of those things when you were born. For her, one child was enough, and she was certain your mother would feel the same way. That or she just wanted to punish Jackie. So much of what your grandmother did felt like punishment because your mother had disappointed her."

Dixon felt a chill. "Grandma was really that rough on Mom?"

"I hate to say it, son, but in many ways, your grandparents made things harder for her than they should've been. Still, Jackie refused to leave with me."

"I...I didn't realize."

"Of course you didn't. We all tried to keep you out of the middle, but it wasn't easy. After I left, I worried what your grandma might be doing to Jackie."

Dixon shook his head. "I knew they fought, but..." He'd always thought the conflict was his mother's fault. After all, she was selfish and self-centered and...all the things Grandma had constantly labeled her.

"Don't be too hard on Jackie, Dix," his father said, as if reading his thoughts. "She did the best she could. We were young, and we made mistakes, but I'll tell you something. She'll always be my first love."

Shocked, Dixon blurted, "I thought you were happy with Lucinda."

Greg chuckled. "I'm very happy with Luci. That doesn't mean I didn't love your mom. In some ways, I'll always love her. That's how first love works. Those who are blessed enough to keep their first love for a lifetime are blessed indeed."

Confused, Dixon could only nod. On one hand, it pleased him that his parents had loved each other. Somehow it made him feel…whole. On the other hand, the idea that his father might still care for his mother felt ominous. What if Jackie played on those feelings? What if she somehow messed up everything? Again. It seemed to him that the best thing he could do was keep his parents apart.

* * *

Fawn said nothing when Dixon again came to the breakfast table dressed for church. She was glad that he attended services regularly, but she could feel only discouragement and dismay when he again walked out without issuing any sort of invitation for anyone to join him. Perhaps she needed to make it clear that Jackie could accompany him if he was willing to give her a little aid. Instead, once more, Fawn and Jackie would have church at home.

After breakfast Fawn carried her laptop and her mother's old Bible into the living room and set both on the coffee table so they could enjoy the fire and the Christmas tree. Holding hands, Jackie led the two of them in prayer, thanking God for His many blessings, praising Him for His goodness and asking for His protection for all their loved ones. Then Fawn logged on to a certain website and picked a favorite teacher, who specifically referenced Joseph's reaction to Mary's pregnancy. With Bella staring cross-eyed at the glow of the Christmas lights, Fawn played the teaching on the computer. She paused it periodically in order to discuss certain points with Jackie, who didn't shy away from using her own personal experience to illustrate her arguments.

"The problem with allowing ourselves to be ruled by emotion," Jackie said, "especially when that emotion is hurt, is that we react from desperation and the belief that we aren't loved. When we choose to react in faith, we're choosing to believe God loves us and to trust that He has our best interests at heart. One way is mindlessly careening through life. The other is calmly letting God lead."

Fawn nodded, realizing that, for all the hurt of her parents' deaths, she had never felt unloved. She could thank her grandmother, her twin and the good Lord for that. Jackie readily admitted that she had pushed away those who loved her, Greg and Dixon, in an effort to win back the love of those she had disappointed, her parents, only to wind up with neither. Harry had helped her see that she could truly find her self-worth in just one place, Christ Jesus.

Jackie had grown so much in her faith that she could see Harry's death as a means of bringing her together with her son. Fawn wondered if Dixon would agree, but she doubted he would have given Jackie the time of day if Harry still lived and her health was not failing.

The question of Bella's future remained unanswered. Surely he would soon realize that he was his sister's rightful caretaker. The idea that he might not hurt Fawn's heart. In fact, as much as she loved the baby and would gladly raise her, the idea of Dixon's rejection of the child depressed Fawn deeply. For that reason, she eagerly agreed when Jackie moved to the upright piano and proposed they sing Christmas carols. What could be more fun?

Jackie's playing was rusty and required a few minutes of practice before they could begin, but what they lacked in expertise, they made up for in enthusiasm. Fawn gave full reign to her husky, throaty alto—until she looked around and realized that Dixon stood behind her in the very center of the room.

"Sounds like I'm missing a good time," he said, a slight smile curling his lips. Fawn quickly looked away, wishing the floor would open and swallow her. Then he said, "You have an amazing voice, Fawn. Where'd you learn to sing like that?"

She shot a glance at him, expecting to see a sarcastic expression despite the sincere tone. Instead, he seemed to mean it. Mumbling that the *Lenape* love to sing, she watched Dixon smile down at the baby sleeping in the carrier.

Saying that she needed to get lunch on the table, Fawn quickly turned away and hurried into the kitchen. On one level, she was pleased to see Dixon forming an attachment to the baby. That was exactly what needed to happen. Yet, she felt a definite heartache. Once she left here, she might never again see Jackie or Bella. Or Dixon. The thought broke her heart.

She was up to her elbows in fried chicken when Dixon came in wearing jeans and a plaid flannel shirt. He leaned a hip against the cabinet next to the stove and crossed his feet at the ankles, hanging the heels of his hands on the counter behind him.

"I didn't mean to embarrass you earlier. I was just surprised to hear singing when I came in."

"You don't sing in church?"

"Of course I do."

"Well, your mother and I had church here this morning."

"I see." For a moment he said nothing more, then, "I should've invited you to come with me this morning."

She didn't let her surprise show. "Why didn't you?"

"I'm not sure what'll happen when my parents meet again."

Caught off guard, she looked away from the frying pan, one hand gingerly grasping a freshly dipped chicken leg. "Oh."

Dixon rubbed his head, sighed and admit-

ted, "Dad knows about her and Bella, but...
I have no idea how it's going to go between
them."

"I know it's awkward. How'd he take it?"

Frowning, Dixon rubbed his ear. "More
calmly than I expected frankly."

Bella squeaked from the other room. Fawn
quickly but carefully laid the chicken leg in
the frying pan and began wiping her hands,
but then she realized that several pieces already needed turning and reached for the
tongs.

"I'll get her," Dixon volunteered.

Before Fawn could think better of that plan,
he walked out of the kitchen. She quickly
took care of the chicken and started preparing a bottle, but the minutes dragged by before he reappeared, Bella cradled in his arms,
her fist crammed into her mouth.

Fawn felt a certain amount of relief accompanied by a kind of warmth at seeing
him there with the baby, but she said only,
"Somebody's hungry."

"That makes two of us," he said, grinning. "That chicken smells amazing."

Flushing with the compliment, Fawn said, "I'll have food on the table in a few minutes."

"I know. Didn't mean to rush you. I've just learned to appreciate your cooking. And everything else you do around here."

She tried to ignore the thrill of that simple compliment. "Uh. Thanks."

"No. Thank you."

"Um. You're welcome."

When she reached for the baby, he took the bottle from her instead, saying, "I think I can manage to feed her. Jackie helped me change her just now, but I got this."

"Ah. Well, um…" Fawn grabbed up a towel and wiped her hands again. "I'll mash these potatoes, then."

Smiling, Dixon nudged Bella's fist out of her mouth with the nipple then laughed as she latched on.

"Be sure not to let air into the nipple," Fawn counseled. "Keep it full of formula. And don't let her suck it dry."

"Okay." He tilted the bottle upward a bit before walking over to the table and pulling out a chair with his foot.

Fawn got busy with the meal, keeping one eye on the preparations and the other on Dixon and the baby. He kept talking to Bella and laughing at her.

"She doesn't let anything get in the way of that bottle, does she? She looks you straight in the eyes like she's talking to you, but all the while she's guzzling down the milk."

"She's really a very good baby," Fawn said. "She was sleeping through the night within three weeks of birth."

"So you've been with them from the very beginning," Dixon surmised.

"I've known your mother—" Fawn had to stop to think "—nearly four years, so yeah, from before the beginning with Bella."

"I didn't realize. I guess I just didn't think it through. I hope Jackie realizes what a good friend you are."

Fawn turned the burner off under her gravy

and turned to face him. "She'd do the same thing for me."

Dixon looked down at Bella and adjusted the bottle. "Good to know. But...too often, Jackie's ordeals are of her own making."

Fawn sighed. "I'm the first to admit that I don't know a lot about men, but Grandmother says that you all listen with your heads too much, that you need women to teach you to hear with your hearts. When your mother and grandmother were fighting, did you never hear the anguish or anger in their words? Did you never hear the disappointment and rejection in your grandmother's criticism? The pain and shame in your mother's recriminations?"

"You can justify almost anything," he argued, focusing on the baby, "but common sense ought to win sometimes."

"Common sense would say that she shouldn't have had Bella. Do you think she shouldn't have had Bella?" Fawn demanded, folding her arms. "The doctors all pressed her to give up the idea of carrying Bella to term, but she insisted, no matter what that meant to her personally. She wouldn't have given up Bella any more than she'd have given up you when everyone but your father demanded she do that!"

He looked stunned, allowing the nipple to slip from the baby's mouth. "What? Who demanded that she give me up?"

Realizing that she'd said too much, Fawn turned back to the stove. "That's not my truth to tell. All I'm saying is that you should open your heart a little. Now, I have to get this food on the table."

Bella squawked, but then she burped loudly as Dixon got to his feet. Before Fawn could turn again, he had carried the baby from the room. Biting her tongue, Fawn wondered if she should follow, but in the end she merely bowed her head and prayed for God to shower both mother and son with wisdom and understanding.

She shouldn't care that she'd probably just destroyed any good opinion of her that Dixon might have formed to this point. But she did care. Much, much more than she should.

Chapter Six

With his hands full of baby and bottle, Dixon couldn't very well knock on his mother's bedroom door, so he simply shouldered it open and went inside. Jackie lay atop the bedcovers, thumbing through the photo album. Dixon didn't beat around the bush.

"Is it true that you were pressured to give me up?"

Jackie jerked around on the bed. When she saw him standing there with Bella, her dismay gave way to a pleading smile. She sat up.

"Don't think too badly of your grandparents for that. I was very young, after all, and they were in shock. I was their little girl, and that was all they could think about just then. It's understandable that their first impulse was for me to give you up for adoption."

For a moment he could hardly breathe. Then Bella squirmed, and he had to readjust to keep from dropping her. Jackie held out her arms. He laid the baby on the bed next to their mother and sat beside her.

"I have a hard time thinking of Grandma and Grandpa not wanting me. They were the one real constant in my life. They loved me."

"We all loved you," Jackie asserted. "That was part of the problem. As soon as you were born, your grandmother wanted to be your mother as much as I did."

"And that's when you regretted having me," he ventured.

"Never!" she exclaimed. "I've never regretted having you or keeping you. I only regret that I wasn't mature enough to handle motherhood and marriage better. It was much more difficult than I'd imagined. I was a spoiled only child, Dix, and when Greg's mother died and his father decided to take a job in Washington, DC, I convinced Greg that if we had a baby, everyone would let us get married and we could stay together. I didn't think beyond that. I didn't consider what it would cost him or me or my parents. I didn't realize how disappointed they would be in me or what it would do to our relationship. The depth of their anger shocked me. But I wouldn't change it because it gave us you. I wish I'd done a lot of things differently, son, but not you."

He nodded and swallowed down the lump in his throat. "I think I understand."

"I'm so proud of how you turned out, Dix, and I have your grandparents to thank for that. I might have felt that they no longer had room left in their lives for me, but I can't fault them for all they did for you."

He looked up sharply at that, realizing suddenly that his grandmother's possessiveness had had another side to it, an exclusivity, as if she'd needed to concentrate her love on one person or thing at a time. Moreover, she'd demanded an exclusive kind of loyalty from those around her. That must have played a part in his parents' divorce, but now he wondered if it had also led him to supplant his own mother in his grandmother's affections.

Did you ever ask yourself why your mother did those things?

Little more than a child herself, Jackie must have felt so bereft, abandoned, unloved in her own home. Yet, he looked at Bella and knew, *knew*, that her presence made no difference at all in how his mother felt about him. He remembered what his father had told him about his grandmother punishing Jackie for disappointing her.

"Mom," he asked carefully, watching Bella clasp his finger with her tiny fist, "why didn't Grandma have any more kids?"

Jackie sniffed and said, "She used to tell me that one perfect child was enough for any mother. But that was before I embarrassed her in front of the whole town."

It was just as his father had said, then, just as he'd feared. One love at a time. So much he hadn't understood. So much he'd never have understood if Fawn hadn't spoken up. He looked at his mother, searching for words. Tears stood in Jackie's eyes. Yet, oddly, she smiled, too. The apology fell out of his mouth.

"I'm sorry. I didn't mean—"

She reached up and pressed her fingertips to his lips, shaking her head. Tears rolled down her thin cheeks even as her smile broadened. "That's the first time you've called me Mom in years."

Before he could apologize for that, too, Fawn called out, "Food's getting cold!"

Jackie hastily wiped her eyes and scooted toward the foot of the bed, saying, "You take your sister. I'll grab the carrier."

Dixon didn't argue, but he waited for her to catch up to him then put the baby into her seat and carried both toward the kitchen.

When they reached the doorway, they found Fawn at the stove, pouring gravy into a bowl. Jackie laid a hand on Dixon's wrist and quietly said, "You don't know how much

I wish I'd been more like her when I first had you. She'd have made the right decisions. Just look at her. So capable and responsible."

"She seems…strong, helpful." Beautiful, kind, loving, wise…

"From an early age," Jackie confirmed, sliding into a chair. "It's how she was raised."

"How who was raised?" Fawn asked, carrying the bowl to the table.

Jackie just smiled, and Dixon said, "Somebody taught you how to cook."

"Can't work at a diner without learning how to cook," Fawn said, "but Grandmother deserves a lot of the credit, too."

"Remind me to thank her," Dixon said, placing Bella's seat on the chair between him and his mother, the table being so heavily laden.

"You could start by thanking God," Jackie suggested, reaching out her hand.

Nodding, Dixon clasped her fingers with his. Then he held out his other hand to Fawn. Her delicate fingers trembled slightly as they met his. He folded them into his hand, felt them calm and warm, bowed his head and began to pray. Something he hadn't felt in a very long while stole over him. Peace. A true measure of real peace.

They enjoyed almost twenty-four hours of complete amity. Fawn had never seen Jackie at such peace, and at the same time she seemed to lose strength with alarming rapidity. She bloomed whenever Dixon was around, and he exerted himself to be charming and kind, calling her "Mom" and "Mama" and playing with Bella, who flirted shamelessly, wiggling her eyebrows and cooing at him. As soon as Dixon left, however, Jackie languished, spending much of her time napping. When Fawn helped her bathe on Monday afternoon, she was alarmed at how thin Jackie had become, despite her swollen ankles and knees.

Fawn hated to disturb the harmony by talking to Dixon about his mother's failing health, but she knew that she must. Unfortunately, the weather turned unexpectedly in the wee hours of Tuesday morning, and they woke to find sleet pelting every surface. Dixon rushed out to hay the cattle in the field and returned a couple hours later with a red nose and a concerned air to phone the local veterinarian, who was already making calls, according to his wife.

"Trouble?" Fawn asked as he pocketed his phone.

Nodding, Dixon pulled out his gloves again. "Got another pregnant heifer in the barn. This one's coughing her lungs up, and the vet can't get here for hours."

"What are you going to do?"

He shook his head. "No clue." He stopped and looked at her. "You got any ideas? That stuff of your grandma's has worked wonders on that wound. I expect the vet to ask about it when he sees the improvement."

Thrilled, Fawn bit her lip to hide her smile and tried to think. "Do you have a vaporizer?"

"Afraid not."

"A boiling teapot then? And camphor?"

"There's a teapot in the cabinet over the refrigerator," he said, "and camphor's in the medicine cabinet, but the stove's in the house and the cow's in the barn." He snapped his fingers. "I've got a camp stove."

"You set that up. I'll bring the teapot, camphor and extra water."

"There's a tap in the barn, and it won't be frozen."

"Excellent."

He hurried off to set up the camp stove. She ran to tell Jackie that she would be out of the house for a while and why. With Bella in her crib and Jackie resting comfortably in the bed in the same room, Fawn rummaged through the medicine cabinet, grabbed the teapot and threw on her coat. She found Dixon in the barn setting up the camp stove just outside the stall near the heifer's head.

"Hopefully the camphor can get into her lungs without burning her eyes," she said, preparing the pot.

He nodded. "I'll hang around long enough

to make sure. I can always put blinders on her, if necessary."

With the filled teapot on the flame, Fawn joined him at the fence wall of the stall, pushing up the sleeves of her coat. "I hope she'll be okay."

"Me, too. I can't afford to lose heifers and calves."

"Wish I could do more."

He shot her a weak smile. "You do more than enough around here. Sometimes I wonder what we'd do without you." Suddenly he turned and looked her over. "Say, where'd you get that coat? You're pretty cute in it, but it's not a woman's coat."

"No, it's not." Smiling, she snuggled down into it. "Harry gave it to me. I got caught at work one day pretty much like today when nobody expected the weather to turn. I was ready to dash to my car and shiver in the cold until it warmed up, but Harry wouldn't hear of it. He took the coat off his own back and gave it to me, insisted I keep it when I remarked that it was warmer than anything I'd ever owned."

"He really was a special guy, wasn't he?"

"Absolutely." She lifted her shoulders, snuggling a little deeper. "I'll always treasure this old coat."

Dixon slid a hand to the back of his head, pushing his hat forward as if to hide his expression. "Wish I hadn't been so stubborn and could've gotten to know Harry."

"What's past is past," Fawn counseled, realizing as she said it that she would do well to heed her own words. Wasn't that essentially what her grandmother had been trying to tell her about her father? Her sister might not agree, but what kind of sense did it make to let her father's weakness overshadow their lives forever? It was one thing to learn from past mistakes, but it was another to let the past control the present and the future.

She took a deep breath and said, "I need to talk to you about your mom."

Dixon looked down. "She's losing ground, isn't she?"

"I'm afraid so. We'll keep praying, but she needs to see a doctor. Soon. If she keeps going as she is, hospice will need to be called in, and that will require a doctor's assistance."

Gulping, Dixon said, "I wonder if we can even get hospice care out here. She might have to go to a facility in Ardmore or Duncan."

"I know she'd rather be here with you and Bella."

"I'd rather have her here."

Well, that was definite progress, so Fawn decided to take the conversation a step further.

"She's made it clear that she wants Bella raised in the country like she was. I've promised her that if I wind up raising Bella, I'll find a way to keep us in the country. Honestly, I can't imagine preferring to live in town, even a small town."

Dixon's jaw had dropped, as if he couldn't believe what he was hearing. "You would consider raising Bella?"

"Seems to me I'll have to if you aren't considering raising her yourself."

He clapped a hand over his mouth then shoved it over his face, pushing back his hat. Obviously, he hadn't thought through to the logical conclusion with Bella, given his mother's health prospects. Fawn wanted to believe that was because he couldn't quite face the idea of his mother's death yet, and she was trying to give him time to come to terms with it. Finally, he shook his head. "I…I don't see how I could possibly raise her. Not alone."

"Single men and women raise children all the time, Dixon," Fawn pointed out gently. "It's not easy, I'm sure, but they find ways to make it work."

"Maybe so," he said, "but…" He shook his head. "I'm not like you, Fawn. I've never had to care for another person in my life. I used to tell my grandpa that I'd always take care of him, but then one day he got mixed up and took too many blood pressure pills and died before anybody could get to him. It was horrible. And at the same time a part of me was relieved, because I don't know how I'd have managed if I'd really had to take care of him."

"You were barely more than a boy then," she pointed out, "and look at all you've accomplished since. I see what you've done, and I've heard your plans and it all shows great strength and promise, Dixon, especially when most men your age are out blowing every cent they get their hands on. You can do this. If you want to."

He just stared at her, until she turned and walked out, trudging back to the house. Had he really not considered what would happen to his baby sister once their mother was gone? Or had he just assumed that Bella would go into foster care and that no one would expect him to step up and take custody of her?

Fawn couldn't believe that he could be so callous as to consign his baby sister to foster care. Maybe he thought she'd be better off adopted. What Fawn wanted to believe was that, however hostile he had seemed at first, Dixon loved Jackie and couldn't quite face the possibility of losing her yet. So far, he'd made sure that Bella had everything she needed, and he regularly interacted with her and Jackie now. Fawn instinctively felt that, deep down, he loved them both and would step up when the time came. He just needed a little more time.

What Fawn feared most now, truthfully, was that she might be falling in love with him, and the wisdom of that remained very much in question.

The vet didn't show until nearly lunch. That gave Dixon time to think. As usual, Fawn was correct. He should be the one to raise Bella if something happened to his mom, but he couldn't imagine how he could swing raising a baby on his own.

Suddenly, he had some idea what his fifteen-year-old mother must have been faced with when he'd been born. Later, as a seventeen-year-old single mom...she must have been overwhelmed, even with her parents to help her. And all these years he'd listened to his grandmother's criticism and punished her for not being the perfect mother. He felt a shocking shame about that now, but some hurt and resentment over his mother's behavior lingered. At some point, shouldn't she have started thinking about *him*?

As predicted, the veterinarian had been interested in Fawn's grandmother's home remedy, and he'd praised Fawn's ingenuity. Dr. Burns politely turned down an invitation to stay for lunch, however, saying that his wife was home cooking even as they spoke and would blister him if he failed to show for the meal.

"She's of the opinion that I work too much," he divulged with a wide smile, "and she's so pregnant that she can barely reach the stove."

Dixon couldn't help wondering if Meredith Burns cooked half as well as Fawn... What was her last name, anyway? He asked as he sat down to the table.

"Ambor."

"Amber?"

"Ambor. *O-R*, not *E-R*."

"Ambor. Does that mean something?"

"No idea. I'm told it's Welsh, but my father's given name was Piero. His mother was Italian, so..." She shrugged.

Dixon chuckled, thinking what an exotic character she was, and wolfed down his food. Worrisomely, his mother didn't come to the table. He was almost glad to find his dad waiting to talk to him about her when he finally got to the house in town.

"I've been thinking, son," Greg said. "You should spend your birthday with your mom this year. I can join you later in the evening with the rest of the family. What do you think?"

The bottom dropped out of Dixon's stomach. "I don't know, Dad. I'm sure Mom would like for me to spend the day with her. Could be awkward, though."

Greg clapped him on the shoulder. "We can make it work."

"I mean, really awkward."

"Come on, son. Have a little faith. None of us are teenagers any longer, and we all love you. If you can't trust your own parents with this, though, trust God. He's got this. Okay?"

All Dixon could say to that was, "Okay."

"Now," Greg said, smiling, "about that soffit in the master bedroom here…"

That started an old argument about wallpaper versus texture and paint. Dixon barely even noticed when he eventually lost.

Chapter Seven

"Today?" Fawn repeated, trying to keep the dismay out of her voice. "His birthday is *today*?" She dropped the dish towel on the counter, asking, "Why didn't you tell me sooner?"

"I never dreamed he'd spend the day here with us, that's why!" Jackie gushed. "Honestly, I was prepared to ignore the whole thing. I thought he'd go off to work as usual then spend the evening with his dad."

As if she could have ignored her son's birthday. Fawn wanted to shake her, but that wouldn't accomplish what needed to be done.

"We need a cake," Fawn thought aloud,

pushing up the sleeves of her tunic, "and presents. And a special meal. What's his favorite?"

Jackie wafted a hand in unconcern. "Anything Mexican. Oh, and he loves chocolate chip waffles. As for cake, his favorite is strawberry."

Strawberry? Just before Christmas? "I have to go into town. I'll go when Dixon goes out to hay the cattle, and I'll take Bella with me. Will the stores be open that early?"

"Store," Jackie corrected. "There's just the grocery, but it carries a little bit of everything. Oh, and the Feed & Supply just outside of town. I suppose they might have something there. Both should be open by seven."

"That's good."

"I have a little money," Jackie said, "and I've noticed that his everyday belt is showing some wear."

"I'll see what I can do."

Beaming, Jackie practically danced out of the kitchen, more energetic than Fawn had seen her in days. Meanwhile, Fawn's mind raced with plans for an impromptu birthday celebration.

At least Dixon took his time coming to the table. That allowed her to have his chocolate chip waffles ready. Thankfully, she found chocolate chips in the freezer. He took one look at his plate and grinned at his mother.

"You remembered."

"Of course I remembered! Happy birthday!"

"I haven't had these in years," he said, digging in. He popped the first drippy triangle into his mouth, and hummed his approval before proceeding to demolish the entire plateful. Afterward, he had a leisurely second cup of coffee then geared up to hay the cattle and take care of the animals in the barn.

"I'm sorry you have to do this on your birthday," Jackie told him, but he just shrugged.

"This ice won't last much longer and the cattle can go back to fending for themselves," he said. "I actually like working with animals, but I can't help worrying about the sick or injured ones."

"That seems right to me," Fawn commented, going to gather up his breakfast things.

"Guess so." He chuckled and set his hat onto his head. He looked quite mature and capable under that hat, as if turning twenty-nine brought gravitas to his character. He also looked pleasantly relaxed and pleased. He passed her on his way to kiss Jackie on the cheek. Then as he headed for the door once more, he said, "Thanks for the waffles." And as naturally as buttoning his coat, he planted a swift kiss on Fawn's cheek, too.

The electric contact knocked them both back. He jerked sideways, and she knocked into the chair. He looked as shocked as she felt.

"Uh. Welc…um… S-sure."

Jackie's snicker made Fawn glare at her, but Dixon put his head down and strode swiftly out the door. Quickly straightening her smile,

Jackie mumbled that she'd get Bella dressed and left the room.

Fawn took a moment to catch her breath then loaded the dishwasher and gathered her things, telling herself the entire time that an off-hand kiss to the cheek meant absolutely nothing. Jackie had Bella ready by the time Fawn had the car warmed up. They went out by the front door just in case Dixon returned sooner than expected. Jackie promised to kick back in the game room recliner and rest there until Fawn returned.

Following the GPS directions on her phone, Fawn drove into War Bonnet. When they'd initially arrived, they'd driven into the ranch from the opposite direction. Jackie had been so tired after the nearly five-hour drive from northeastern Oklahoma that Fawn had seen no reason to continue into the tiny town, especially as they'd come well provisioned, thanks to her grandmother.

The community lived up to its billing. About two city blocks long, it offered just two retail establishments, a diner and the grocery, not counting the Feed & Supply just outside the city limits. Fawn went to the Feed & Supply first. She filled up her car with gas at the station on the corner then parked, took Bella from her safety seat and carried the baby inside the store in front of the massive silos.

To her surprise, she found some nice leather goods on offer. She'd noticed that Dixon had no hatband, so she bought that. The heavily tooled belt had a smooth place in the back for embossing, but the belt would have to be sent away for that particular service. The hatband was a simple plain leather strip, but it matched the belt in color.

She also took the opportunity to buy three small items as Christmas gifts, a pair of tiny moccasins for Bella, a bookmark embossed with a cross for Jackie and a handsome, protective watchband for Dixon. Imagining his surprise on Christmas day pleased her. She just couldn't let the holiday pass without gifting him in some way, letting him know in some measure that she cared.

The grocery yielded cards and wrapping paper, as well as everything necessary to bake a strawberry cake with strawberry buttercream frosting. The berries themselves weren't great, but to her surprise she found chocolate in which to dip them. More surprising still, in a case in the front of the building she found a package of faux turquoise stones set in silver studs perfect for leatherwork. She didn't have her leatherworking tools with her, but she could carve and split the leather with a sharp knife if she was careful. The trick was going to be keeping Dixon out of the way while she worked. Still, it was a small project.

Finishing her purchases, she hurried out to the car, clicked Bella's carrier into the safety apparatus, stowed her goods and drove back to the ranch. Dixon met her at the door, scowling as he took Bella's carrier from her.

"I could have made that trip into town for you."

"No, no," she said, turning back to the car.

"It's your birthday. Get Bella to your mom, will you?"

He frowned, but he did as she asked. When he dashed out to the car to help haul in the purchases a few moments later, she had the important bags in hand and was able to take care of them herself without him being any the wiser. She quickly stashed what she needed to keep hidden then prepared a bottle for Bella, which she dispatched a few minutes later with him. She got the cake in the oven, then joined the others in the game room, where Jackie and Dixon were playing a board game while Bella slept in her carrier.

Chuckling at the colored money and property deeds scattered across the game table, she shook her head. "Really?"

"You'd think she'd let me win on my birthday, but nothing doing," Dixon complained good-naturedly.

"Yeah, right now it's a draw. We see how much pity you have on your poor, sick mama."

Fawn went over and picked up the remote

to the sizable flat-screen television on the wall. "Maybe when you get tired of that, you'll watch a movie," she suggested. Pointing the remote, she turned on the set and went through the steps to download a movie. When she found a certain title, Dixon exclaimed, "Oh, man, I love that one! Haven't seen it in years."

Fawn started the download. "It'll be ready when you are. I'll bring in lunch later. First, though, I'll put Bella Jo to bed."

She picked up the carrier with the baby, who reacted with a deep sigh.

"Sometimes I wonder if that kid's deaf," Dixon remarked lightly. "She can sleep through anything."

"She's not deaf," Jackie assured him, sounding amused. "She's just acclimated to having sound around her."

"Where she came from, she had to be," Fawn remarked.

"Where was that?" he asked.

"My grandmother's."

"Rebecca Weller's is a household of

women," Jackie said, "and you know what they say about women." Dixon shook his head. "Research says the average woman speaks twenty thousand words per day, while men use seven thousand on average."

He pointed at Fawn and said, "Well, this one is way below average then."

Jackie laughed. "Her twin makes up for it!"

"Then I'm glad I got the right twin," Dixon quipped, grinning at Fawn.

They were still discussing the matter when a blushing Fawn left the room. She quickly got to work on the hatband, which was very simple, then managed to show it to Jackie when she carried in lunch a little later. Jackie gave her an enthusiastic two thumbs-up when Fawn whispered that she wanted to do a similar thing on the belt.

Dixon remarked that something smelled great. Thinking quickly, Fawn replied that it must be popcorn, though she hadn't yet popped any. "Can't watch a movie without popcorn, right? I forgot to ask. With or without butter?"

The suggestion worked.

"With," he answered. "Definitely."

"Coming right up."

She hurried back to the kitchen and popped the popcorn, which covered the aroma of strawberry cake nicely. Between that, dipping the strawberries to decorate the cake, embedding the stones in the belt, sneaking a peek at Jackie, getting everything wrapped and starting dinner, she didn't even hear the baby until Dixon showed up with her in the kitchen.

"Somebody's ready for a bo— What's all this? Wow. Look at that cake!"

Fawn turned from placing the last strawberry atop the cake, flicked off the burner under the rice and lifted both arms. Really, she was surprised she'd gotten this far with the arrangements. "This is…your birthday."

He glanced around. "You didn't have to do this."

"Your mom wanted you to have a real birthday."

"That smells like Mexican food."

"Nothing fancy. Tacos and rice."

He grinned. "I really did get the right twin." Suddenly he smacked himself in the head with the heel of one hand. "Oh, no. I should've told you sooner. My dad and the rest of the family are coming over."

That information widened her eyes. "When?"

"Soon."

Closing her eyes, she pinched the bridge of her nose. This last-minute stuff was getting to be a habit. "Yeah, that information would have been nice to hear, like, two hours ago. Or yesterday."

He grimaced. "Sorry. I didn't think about dinner."

"Obviously."

"Put it back. We'll eat after they leave."

She shook her head, thinking of Jackie. "I'll…" Inspiration struck. "I'll make a dip of the rice and taco meat, throw down some chips and tortillas, put together a salad." She tapped her chin. "I think I can come up with queso, and there's salsa. We'll serve it buffet style." She spread her hands. "It'll have to do."

"Sounds fine," he said, smiling. He nodded at the two-layer cake topped with chocolate-covered strawberries. "At least we have plenty of cake. Strawberry is my favorite."

"Jackie told me," she said, her irritation fading in the face of his delight. "Take Bella to your mom while I fix a bottle then come help me get this all on the table."

He did as instructed, carrying dishes to and from the dining table as Fawn prepared them. She was pouring corn chips from the bag into a bowl when a knock landed on the front door. Dixon glanced at her before going to answer it. Only when she looked over to find Jackie standing in the doorway to the game room did Fawn realize that Dixon had also failed to inform his mother that they were to have guests. She thought Jackie would faint dead away when Greg Lyons stepped through that door.

It had to be Greg Lyons. No one else could look that much like Dixon, from the hairline and eyebrows to the lay of his ears and curve of his jaw. Fawn had thought Dixon resembled Jackie until she saw Greg, but no one could doubt who had fathered Dixon Lee Lyons.

Fortunately, Jackie pulled herself together. She even managed to look as if she was lounging in the doorway rather than leaning against it for support. Dixon shot his mom an apologetic, slightly panicked look before turning a bright smile on his father and those crowding in behind him. Fawn saw a tallish, slender woman with long dark, curly hair and rimless glasses. Two boys, very much like Dixson but with sharper features and darker hair, stood directly behind her. Both had bright blue eyes and were tall, one of them taller than Dixon and their father. Neither were quite as broad-shouldered. They stared at Jackie with open curiosity.

Dixon threw his arms wide then pointed to the table. "Hope you're hungry! Fawn's laid out a buffet. And wait until you see the cake!"

All eyes swung to the table—and landed on Fawn. Greg's eyebrows went straight up. His wife beamed. The boys, for Fawn could see that they were only teenagers, bugged their eyes and started elbowing each other. Bella squawked just then, and Jackie took control of the situation.

"Son, would you bring your sister in to meet everyone? I've changed her, so at least she's dry. If not as presentable as I'd like."

Dixon blushed, red creeping up from his throat to his cheeks. He flashed a weak smile around the room, bobbed his head and rushed over to slide past his mother and into the game room. Fawn offered up her own smile, which felt none too robust, and went forward with outstretched hands.

"Can I take your coats?"

People immediately began shedding their outerwear. Greg wore a heavy jean jacket lined with sheepskin. His wife handed over a long brown wool coat, beneath which she wore plain jeans and a simple red sweater.

She kept her large, patchwork leather bag with her. The boys both wore leather. The taller one offered to help her with the coats.

"She doesn't need help, Bass," Dixon barked, re-entering the room with Bella nestled in the crook of one arm.

Because she was practically staggering under the weight of the men's coats, Fawn sent him a frown, then she upended it when she faced his brother again. "Thank you, anyway. And please help yourself to the food."

Bass grinned, and, oh, was he going to be a lady-killer in his day.

She turned to carry the coats to the bedroom, scowling at Dixon when he scowled at her. Lucinda was making goo-goo eyes at Bella, while Greg homed in on Jackie. Fawn prayed that Jackie wouldn't let pride get the better of her. She needed to sit down and relax. Hopefully Dixon had sense enough to realize that. But then he hadn't had sense enough to warn her that his father would be showing up with his family in tow!

Dumping the coats on her own bed, Fawn hurried back to the living room to find Jackie sitting on the couch with Bella in her arms, the current Mrs. Lyons next to her, Greg occupying the chair at the end of the couch, Dixon nervously hovering over the lot of them and the boys grazing the table in the dining area. When Fawn joined them, Dixon finally realized he hadn't made the necessary introductions.

"Uh, Fawn, I don't think you've properly met my... Everyone. Fawn Ambor. And this, of course, is my father, Greg Lyons, and my st—" He shot a glance at his mother. "Uh, Lucinda Lyons. And those two knuckleheads over there stuffing their faces are my brothers, Bass and Phillip." He relaxed marginally as everyone smiled and nodded, adding, "You really ought to eat something, Dad. Fawn's a great cook."

"I look forward to it," Greg said, staying right where he was.

"You're a nice surprise, Fawn," Lucinda

told her, smiling. "We didn't know Dix had a girlfriend."

Shocked at the assumption, Fawn leaped to correct it, but not before Dixon did.

"Oh, we hardly know each other."

"I'm here with Jackie. I drove her and Bella down from Miami, Oklahoma."

"She's helping out," Dixon said, as if she hadn't made it plain enough.

"Fawn and her family have been the dearest friends I've ever had," Jackie said, smiling smugly.

Lucinda's face colored. "My mistake. It's just you're so much closer to his age than... Well, it's his birthday and..."

"And you're so hot," one of the boys said with a chortle.

Greg coughed, and Dixon made a strangling sound deep in his throat. Fawn didn't know who was more embarrassed, her, Lucinda or Dixon. Her face burned so red that the room suddenly felt ten degrees warmer.

Glancing around blindly, her thoughts

spinning, she said, "Excuse me. I think I forgot to set out drinks."

She turned and walked into the kitchen, unaware that Dixon had followed until she abruptly stopped and he bumped into her. She knew instinctively that it was him, and her temper flared as hot as her embarrassment.

Jerking around, she speared him with an angry glare. "This is all your fault! You embarrassed us all! Shame on you, Dixon Lyons!"

She knew her anger was unreasonable. He hadn't introduced her as his girlfriend. Apparently, he hadn't mentioned her at all! And why should he? She was just his mother's friend. Maybe she'd thought she was becoming his friend, too, but obviously her assumptions were as faulty as Lucinda Lyons's. Except Lucinda's were probably more reasonable.

Fawn realized how it must have seemed to everyone, and she realized, too, that what lay beneath her anger was a deep well of hurt that Dixon had never considered her as anything more than his mother's friend.

While she couldn't help wanting to be so much more.

Chapter Eight

Taken aback by Fawn's anger, Dixon mentally reeled.

"Me?" he whispered back heatedly. "What did I do? I didn't tell anyone you were my girlfriend."

"You didn't tell anyone anything, period! You didn't tell them about me. You didn't tell me or your mother that they were coming. What did you think *that* was going to accomplish?"

"I didn't think!" he admitted, keeping his voice low. "If you must know, I've been reeling since the day I walked in and found you standing in my kitchen!" She sighed, and he immediately regretted those words. "That's not your fault. None of this is your fault."

"Then whose fault is it, Dixon? Your mom's?"

"No. This current mess, tonight, is my fault. I was so nervous about it I didn't handle any of it well. The rest is just…life, I guess." He could blame his grandparents, but in their own way they'd done their best by him. He could blame his parents, but they'd been so young that their mistakes must surely be forgiven. He couldn't help blaming himself in some ways, but there was so much he hadn't known, and what good did it do? One thing was certain, though. "Absolutely none of it is your fault. And you have every reason to be mad at me."

Sighing again, she smoothed a hand down his arm, as if smoothing ruffled feelings. She'd become such a large part of the household.

"I can't be mad at you," she was muttering. "It's your birthday."

She stood there, looking up at him through

her lashes, and he found himself wondering why she *wasn't* his girlfriend. Maybe she wouldn't want to be, but he'd like her to be. Oh, yes, he would. In fact, if Bass flirted with her again, he was going to wind up busting his little brother's nose. He grinned at the thought. Bass was no longer a helpless kid; he'd likely give as good as he got. How long had it been since they'd tussled? Well, it wasn't going to be over this dark-haired beauty.

What would she do if he kissed her, really kissed her? He'd been wondering that a lot lately, but this was not the moment to find out. Soon, though. The idea was beginning to take up a remarkable amount of space in his thoughts and hopes.

"Let me help you get the drinks out," he offered softly.

She nodded and gave him directions. As they carried everything into the dining area and placed them on the table, Dixon became aware of a strange quiet. Glancing around, he saw his brothers standing silently with their plates in their hands. Beyond them, his stepmother sat with Bella in her lap, while his father knelt on one knee in front of his mother.

Jackie and Greg held hands, and both bowed their heads as Greg softly led the three adults in prayer. Astounded, Dixon could only stare, such feelings coming over him that he momentarily felt paralyzed. It was as if the world slowly righted in that moment, as if some missing piece in the puzzle of his life carefully settled into place. After the prayer, Greg stretched up and kissed Jackie on the forehead, while Luci reached over and patted her knee and Jackie mopped her eyes. Dixon's own eyes filled, and he knew then that God had given him everything he needed to take care of Bella and see that Jackie lived the rest of her life in joy, however long that might be. He looked at his mother and, to his shame, knew that if she had not been ill, he'd have turned her away. Yes, she had made poor choices, but who hadn't?

Beside him, Fawn whispered, "Happy birthday."

Swallowing back the tears, he slid his arm about her shoulders, pulling her into his side. She looped her own arm about his waist. He looked at his parents and his baby sister, his brothers standing in respect, the fire warming his hearth, the table laden with all his favorites and the Christmas lights twinkling on the tree. He felt the woman at his side, and thought this was the most perfect moment of his life. Then, in a blink, something surged through him.

It was as if the accounts had suddenly balanced in one part of his life and a new ledger had opened. Suddenly all was right in his old world, and he was ready for the new. He was ready for more. For her. Fawn. He looked down at the dark head of the woman at his side and knew she was exactly where she belonged, where he needed her.

One thing at a time, he told himself.

Aloud he said, "Will you guys eat so I can have cake?"

His dad chuckled and pushed up to his feet. "Good idea."

Fawn slipped away to fill a plate for Jackie and take Bella from Luci so she could eat. Dixon helped himself to the food and sat next to his mother, laughing and talking with his family, every vestige of discomfort banished. Fawn fed Bella then passed her to Jackie and ate her dinner before insisting that Dixon cut the cake. There were no candles to blow out, but Dixon didn't mind.

Fawn made sure that everyone's cup was kept filled, and when Bella fell asleep in her mother's arms, Fawn put the baby to bed. Then, to his surprise, Jackie announced that she had something for him. Fawn produced two small packages. The first was a leather hatband with a turquoise cross twice as tall as the band itself.

He opened the second gift to find a finely tooled leather belt. Embedded in the back were the same turquoise stones in the shapes of his initials, with a small cross on each side. "These are amazing. Where did you get them?"

"Fawn did it," Jackie announced.

"Only the stones, and I found them already set. I just embedded them in the leather of the belt, which we bought just as it is."

"So you do leatherwork?" Luci asked, taking the belt and examining it.

"Sometimes."

"This is very fine work."

"It's simple stuff."

"We have a gift, too," Greg said, nodding at Luci, who pulled a cardboard tube from her large bag and handed it to Dixon.

He tore away the paper and popped the end off the tube to pull out and unroll a magnetic film sign. When he held it up, the legend could clearly be read, "Lyons and Son Construction."

"Dad?"

"We all agree you've earned it," Greg said, nodding at Bass and Phil, "and when these two get older, if they want to come aboard, we'll become Lyons and Sons. Plural. Meanwhile, you're the junior partner."

Dixon laughed. "Wow. Talk about your red-letter days."

Jackie smiled up at him, looking tired and wan. "I'm so proud of you, son."

"That makes all of us, then," Greg announced. "Now, I think it's time to go."

As Fawn hurried off to bring everyone's coats, Lucinda said she was going to have to talk to Fawn about an idea she had for an online leather goods store, and the boys wondered if they could get her to inlay belts for them.

A few moments later Greg asked Dixon, "Why don't you bring Jackie, Fawn and the baby to church with you on Sunday?"

Dixon looked at his mom, who said nothing. "I'm not sure Mom's up to it."

"We could borrow a wheelchair from Wes Billings."

"Why does Wes have a wheelchair?" Jackie asked.

"He had a real battle with cancer last year," Dixon told her, "but he's all right now."

"I'm hearing that he's dating our lady doctor," Greg put in.

"Well, that's fine," Jackie said. "His wife's been gone a long time. I'm happy for him."

"With all his kids married and back home, I'm kind of surprised," Luci remarked, "but I think it's a good thing."

"All three of the Billings kids are back here?" Jackie asked. "Oh, wow. I think I would like to go to church on Sunday, Dix," she said just as Fawn returned with the coats.

"I'll talk to Wes," Greg said.

"We'll get it done," Dixon promised. Then he looked at Fawn, noted her approving smile and knew they'd all made great progress this night.

His dad had been right to suggest this, but Fawn had made it all happen. She'd made the whole day extraordinary. And now, with a junior partnership in the business and the ranch, maybe he was ready to take on more. He knew he could cope with Jackie and Bella now. As for Jackie, that was truly in God's hands. Now all he needed was the courage to reach for what he wanted. Did he dare?

Suddenly, his father's words ran through his head.

Those who are blessed enough to keep their first love for a lifetime are blessed indeed.

Some things, Dixon decided, smiling down at Fawn, were worth the risk. Maybe, just maybe, this would be a very merry Christmas, after all.

Wes Billings showed up at the house late Thursday afternoon with a wheelchair and one Dr. Alice Shorter, a curvy, middle-aged blonde who clutched his arm and beamed up at him as if he'd hung the moon. Fawn thought he was certainly tall enough to have done so. Jackie teased him about his white hair then told him how happy she was that he'd beaten cancer.

"It takes five years to proclaim a cure," Dr. Shorter pointed out.

Billings patted her hand affectionately. "Alice is still learning how faith works."

"Alice is a doctor who has protocols to follow," she retorted. "But I trust that in four more years I'll be proclaiming him cured."

Billings grinned and hugged her before changing the subject. "You know, Jackie, when I was ill, the elders of the church laid hands on me and prayed for me. Would you like that? It can be arranged for Sunday. It seems a fitting thing to do on Christmas Eve."

"I'd like that very much."

"I'll take care of it. Now, will you let Alice examine you?"

"Gladly. I brought my medical records with me, by the way."

Dr. Shorter took her time studying the file and examining Jackie while Fawn served Wes coffee in the kitchen. Afterward, Dr. Shorter changed a couple of Jackie's medications and set her up for a test and an office appointment the week after Christmas. She called the others back into the room as she examined Bella, then pronounced her healthy and adorable, before saying to Jackie, "You took your life into your own hands by bringing her into this world."

"I believe God will honor that," Wes said. "Only He knows why or how He chooses to heal, or why or how He chooses to prolong life, but I believe with all my heart that He will honor your decision to risk your life in order to give life to your daughter."

"He already has," Jackie told him, smiling. "In ways I could barely imagine."

Fawn knew that Jackie was thinking of Dixon, who seemed so much more relaxed and happy since his birthday on Wednesday. He was so effortlessly affectionate with Jackie lately Fawn doubted he even realized what he was doing, but Jackie was blooming. Fawn had to restrain herself to keep from hugging him for it.

As if summoned by her thoughts, Dixon pulled up in his pickup truck with the new signs attached to the doors, parked and came into the house to shake hands with Wes and Dr. Shorter.

"I hear you're going to be a grandpa again."

"Any day now," Wes confirmed, beaming. "Meri says Stark is the calmest father-to-be on earth. Of course, he's a doctor himself, albeit an animal doctor, and he's been through this before, though, sadly, he lost his first wife and daughter in a car wreck."

"That's tough. He sure seems happy now."

"Babies are something to be happy about," Jackie said, juggling Bella, who had recently learned to grab noses.

"Yeah, they sure are," Dixon agreed, smiling down at the two of them. "Thanks so much for coming out," Dixon said, shaking hands again, "and we'll see you on Sunday."

After they left Fawn explained about the new prescription. Dixon promised to take care of it the next day then said he had some work to do after dinner. He washed up, but didn't shower before he sat down to the table, and as soon as he finished his meal, he announced that he'd be in the barn.

Fawn cleaned up the kitchen, saw to it that the baby was fed and down for the evening, watched TV with Jackie for a while then helped her friend into bed, and still Dixon had not returned to the house. She called her grandmother, reporting that things seemed to be settled there. Dixon had a support system in his father's family and had formed deep bonds with his mother and sister. She couldn't believe that he would not step up in a big way to make a home and take care of Jackie and Bella. He was going to have to hire some help, but that shouldn't be an insurmountable hurdle.

"So, *Mamalis*, you will speak to him about this, and then you will come home. Yes?"

Yes. That was the natural progression. So why was she putting off the conversation?

"It won't get easier if you put it off," her grandmother counseled quietly, as if reading her mind.

"I know, Grandmother. You're right. I'll speak to him tonight."

"Perhaps we will see you for Christmas, after all."

The bottom seemed to drop out of Fawn's stomach. "Perhaps."

She missed her grandmother and her sister, but less than she had expected to. It was easy to see why. She had been so busy, and Jackie and Bella had become family to her. And her foolish heart had loved where it should not.

The sandpaper rasped swiftly over the walnut, smoothing and highlighting the grain of the wood. He'd carved a rose into the top. With different colors of stain, he'd detail it, make it stand out beautifully.

The animals shifted, warning him that he was about to have company just before the door opened and Fawn stepped in on a gust of cold air. He glanced around to be sure that what needed to be covered was. For good measure, as Fawn drew near he reached over and dropped a boxed teddy bear onto the bench seat top of the toy box he'd built for Bella.

"Can we talk?"

"Sure." He smiled, unable to hide his pleasure at seeing her. "What's up?"

"Am I right in thinking that you've made up your mind to let Jackie stay and raise Bella yourself?"

He dusted his hands and started brushing his clothes. "You know I have." Oh, why be embarrassed or disingenuous about it? "It's not just the right thing to do, it's what I want to do."

Fawn smiled. "Good. Good. You must realize then that you're going to have to hire someone to help out around here permanently."

"I've been thinking about that." And her. Who better to take care of things around here? And the arrangement had the added benefit of keeping her right where he wanted her. He hadn't thought of paying her, but why not, at least in the short-term?

She bit her lip then said, "That's good. Okay, then." She tilted her head, looking past him to the temporary worktable he'd set up. "What's that?"

He stepped aside, inviting her to peruse his work. She looked at the top first and then the box.

"Mom has a photo album that'll fit right here," he explained, touching a space within the rosewood box, "and the larger area is for whatever else she wants to put inside."

"A memory box."

"That's right."

"It's beautiful."

Pleased, he had to tuck his hands into his back pockets to keep from reaching for her. "I haven't stained it, but that won't take long."

"And a toy box!" she exclaimed, shifting her focus. "You built that, too?"

"That's what carpenters do. Bella's not old enough to appreciate it yet, but there's a rattle in the box with the bear, and the rest is ready when she needs it."

"It's perfect. All of it."

"I'm glad you think so. Because if you do, Mom will."

"No doubt of it." Fawn turned and strode toward the door, only to turn and say, "I was so worried at first, but you've really stepped up, Dixon. I'm so pleased I could…" She threw up her hands, declaring, "I could kiss you!"

He relaxed back against the worktable, trying not to betray the sudden pounding of his heart. "So what's stopping you?"

She blinked at him, as if trying to figure out exactly what he'd said, maybe what she'd said. Then her eyes grew round, and he could see how she caught her breath, but she didn't turn and run. She just stood there, her fingers opening and closing while she apparently debated how to do this or *whether* to do this. When she took a single step forward, he decided that was signal enough and walked toward her, clasping her face in his hands and turning it up to his.

He didn't have to bend as far as he thought he would, but when their lips met, he wrapped an arm around her waist and easily lifted her onto her tiptoes. Her arms slid around his neck, and she leaned into him.

Yes, he thought. The kiss was exactly right. Everything he'd dreamed it would be and more.

Those who are blessed enough to keep their first love for a lifetime are blessed indeed.

Such elation shot through Dixon that he wanted to laugh. Then he realized that he was laughing, and so was Fawn, her lips trembling against his, their noses snuggled together.

Sighing with satisfaction, he let her down to stand on the soles of her feet. So happy he could barely contain himself, he chuckled and put his forehead to hers, asking, "Does it feel to you as if the elephant just left the room?"

For a moment she said nothing. Then she turned her head, saying, "Something like that. I…I need to get back to the house now. In case the baby wakes."

He nodded and reluctantly released her. "I have to finish up here."

She slipped away. He went to the toy box, lifted the seat and reached inside for the other small box he'd made. He'd asked his mom for suggestions before constructing this, but he wished now that he'd gone to the jewelry store instead. He imagined Fawn's face when she saw this. He'd wanted to give her something to let her know how he felt about her. The ring could come later. Provided she felt the same way.

Chapter Nine

Sunday felt festive, happy and relaxed. For everyone but Fawn. Though tired after church and the short prayer service, Jackie looked better than she had in a long while, a combination of faith, the new medication and sheer happiness. When Greg and his family invited them all over to celebrate Christmas Eve, Jackie seemed eager to accept, and Fawn knew that was the end of her sojourn in War Bonnet.

Jackie, Bella and Dixon had all the support they needed. Lucinda and Greg Lyons would fill in until Dixon had hired permanent help. That left Fawn free to return home and spend Christmas with her own family, free to escape her growing folly. After that kiss, she dared not stay. To do so would be to hopelessly indulge the love that she felt for Dixon, a love she had no real reason to believe he returned.

He had as much as admitted that acknowledging their mutual attraction had allowed him to put it aside.

Does it feel to you as if the elephant just left the room?

He might as well have said, "Well, now that that's out of the way, we can forget about it."

But she would never be able to do that. It was time to go and with as little fanfare as possible. Otherwise, she risked betraying herself. So she quietly packed her bags, and when the moment came to leave for the Lyons family home, she begged off.

"The boys make you uncomfortable," Dixon guessed apologetically.

"A little," she admitted, "but mostly, there are things I need to do. Alone."

He seemed disappointed or maybe just irritated. She couldn't trust her own judgment where he was concerned. At any rate, he didn't argue, just swept out to the warming truck and belted Bella into her safety apparatus. Jackie seemed almost sad, as if she knew this would be the last time she'd see Fawn. Reaching up from her wheelchair, she smoothed a hand over Fawn's cheek.

"Are you sure?"

"Very."

Jackie held her gaze until Fawn turned a kiss into the older woman's palm. Then Jackie nodded and whispered, "Merry Christmas, my sweet friend."

"Merry Christmas, and God bless you."

"He already has. In so many ways, you included."

Dixon returned then, looking almost angry, and wheeled Jackie out of the house. Fawn watched as he helped Jackie into the truck and stowed the chair in the bed. She watched as they drove away, the taillights of the truck fading into black. Working after everyone else had gone to bed, she had managed to decorate Bella's moccasins, Jackie's bookmark and Dixon's watchband. She placed the wrapped packages beneath the tree. Then she quickly loaded her things into her car, called her grandmother to tell her that she would be home by midnight, left the note on her pillow and set out, trying not to think about missing the looks on their faces when they opened her gifts.

She felt a twinge of guilt at leaving this way, but she told herself that she was sparing everyone the awkwardness of a teary farewell. Besides, she didn't trust herself not to weaken at the last moment and stay on just a little while longer, then just a little longer after that and then a few more days until... what? Until one day Dixon brought home a bride or she betrayed her feelings for him and he *asked* her to go, if only to spare them more embarrassment?

Her last sight of the ranch house was in her rearview mirror. Odd how bright and far the lights of a Christmas tree could shine in the gloom of night, even with tears blurring her vision.

"Gone? What do you mean, gone?" Dixon demanded, his hands parked at his waist as he stared down at his mother. They'd had a lovely Christmas Eve celebration. Everyone had been so warm and welcoming that he had been able to forget, for several minutes at a time, his disappointment at Fawn's absence. He'd been planning a private gift exchange the moment he returned to the house. Then they'd found her car missing and the house empty!

"You read the note. She decided to spend Christmas with her family. She's gone."

"When will she be back?"

"I doubt she will," Jackie told him gently.

Panic twisting through him, he threw up a hand. "She can't do that! We need her here!"

"Do we?" Jackie asked, looking up at him from the wheelchair. "You don't think we can manage on our own, at least until we can hire daytime help?"

Dixon frowned. "Don't you want her here?"

"Of course I do. I love the girl. But she knows that."

Fawn knew that *Jackie* loved her. He felt his heart beating in his throat and saw the unspoken advice in his mother's eyes. "Are you saying it would make a difference if she knew that I love her?" he asked baldly.

"Do you?" Jackie returned, obviously trying not to smile.

He didn't even try to finesse it. "Of course I do! The only question is what I should do about it."

Jackie took his hand in hers. "All I can tell you is that I let love leave me once, and I've regretted it ever since. That's why, when it came a second time, I grabbed on with both hands and didn't let go."

And he had condemned her for it. Grown, working with his dad, living with his grandfather, fully capable of caring for himself, and he'd acted as if his mommy had abandoned him on a street curb. Shame joined the panic.

He went to one knee. "I'm so sorry for the way I acted when you met Harry."

"Oh, son."

He held up a hand. "I'm sorry I didn't get to know him. I'm sorry I pushed you away. That's what really happened. You didn't abandon me. I pushed you away. I just didn't understand."

"I know. Now you do."

Nodding, he clapped his hand to the back of his neck. "How do I find her?"

Jackie took out her phone, looked up Fawn's contact information and shared it with Dixon. He stared at the information when it appeared on the screen of his own phone, seeing the address below the phone number. Then he began thumbing through his own contact information.

"Are you going to call her?"

He shook his head and a moment later the call was answered. "Dad," he said, "could you guys come over here? I have to leave town. It's important." When he hung up, Jackie beamed at him.

"It's not an easy place to find. I'll draw you a map while you shave."

He ran a hand over his rough jaw and hurried to his room. His dad and Luci arrived just as he rushed into the living room minutes later. He went to the Christmas tree and found the package he'd wrapped for Fawn. He found, too, a package from her to him. Without a pause, he unwrapped it, revealing a leather watchband set with turquoise stones to match his hatband and belt. Praying that was a good sign, he tucked it into his pocket, then rose to leave.

"Here," Jackie said, holding out her fist. When he put out his hand, she dropped a folded piece of paper and a ring into it, a white gold band with a nice-sized diamond flanked on two sides by smaller ones. "My engagement ring from Harry. I tried to sell it but couldn't get near what it's worth, and Fawn has always liked it. I thought I'd leave it to her, but this way is much better."

Beaming, Dixon kissed her cheek. Then

he paused long enough to look at his parents and say, "Thank you."

Smiling, Greg said, "Merry Christmas."

"Please, God," Dixon breathed, heading out the door. He talked to God for the next five hours.

His muscles felt tied in knots by the time he found Fawn's grandmother's place. It was technically Christmas morning, but pitch-dark outside. Nevertheless, much to Dixon's relief, a light shone in the window of the high-roofed cabin nestled in the evergreens. Pulling into the yard—the cabin and small outbuildings sat too close to the winding road to allow for anything approximating an actual driveway—Dixon noted that Fawn's little auto sat next to two others. Recalling that his mother and sister had resided here for months, he marveled. The porch was barely deep enough for the trio of folding lawn chairs that sat to one side of the plank door, and the house itself didn't look large enough for three people, let alone five, even if one of them was an infant.

After taking the package from the seat beside him, he climbed the steps and crossed the shallow porch to the front door, said another quick prayer and knocked. Mere seconds later the door swung open.

The woman standing there in sweats and bare feet, her long, black hair in a ponytail, looked exactly like Fawn but wasn't. Before she could speak, he said, "I'm looking for your sister."

The dark slashes of her eyebrows, so like Fawn's, lifted. Then she folded her arms as she looked him over. "You must be Dixon Lyons."

"That's right. Can I talk to her?"

"Why should I let you talk to my sister?"

"Why shouldn't you?"

"It's the middle of the night, for one thing."

"Look, I've been driving for hours. Will you tell Fawn I'm here?"

Her eyes narrowed. "Do you drink alcohol, Dixon Lyons?"

"Never developed a taste for it. Just tell her I've come."

"Who's looking after Jackie and Bella?"

"My family. Am I going to have to start yelling for Fawn to come out?"

From behind her twin, he heard Fawn's voice ask, "What's going on?"

"I've brought some things you left behind," Dixon said, and watched as Fawn elbowed her sister out of the way.

"Dixon!" He had to work to keep from smiling at the sight of her, still fully dressed. "Is Jackie okay?"

"As okay as before you disappeared."

She dropped her gaze. "I explained."

"Uh-huh. But you didn't let me explain."

"There's nothing more to say," she said, lifting her chin but not her gaze. "You have everything well in hand now."

"I do," he agreed. "That's not the point. You don't even give a guy a chance."

"For what?"

"*Mamalis*," said another voice, "we don't keep company standing outside in the cold, particularly not on Christmas."

"Yes, Grandmother." Obediently, Fawn

stepped to the side, gesturing for Dixon to enter the building.

The warmth shocked him. He glanced around, surprised by the narrow staircase against the far wall. It couldn't lead anywhere but to a loft. They'd tucked a straggly Christmas tree beneath it. The overall decor seemed a cross between a lodge style and an Ozark theme with Native American touches. What most intrigued him, however, was the tiny woman standing in the door to what was obviously a kitchen. She wore bunny slippers and a gingham wrapper over a heavy flannel nightgown. Except for the silver streaks in her long black hair, she looked far too young to be anyone's grandmother, and she couldn't have stood more than ten inches over four feet. Nevertheless, her authority filled the house.

"Merry Christmas, Mr. Lyons," she said. "Would you like some coffee?"

Dixon smiled. "Very much. Thank you, ma'am, and Merry Christmas to you."

Nodding, she signaled for Dawn to join her, saying, "I will have herbal tea, *Petapan*."

Clearly irritated, Dawn shot a glance at her twin and followed their grandmother into the other room. Smiling to himself, Dixon turned to face the woman he'd chased halfway across the state.

From the moment she'd first seen him standing there on the porch, Fawn hadn't quite been sure what to do with her hands. They kept wanting to reach out for him, but her mind spun with so many thoughts that she couldn't work out why he was here.

"What was it I left behind?"

"This, for one thing," he said, holding out a wrapped gift.

She flushed. "You didn't come all this way to bring me that."

"Just take it."

She couldn't think of a gracious way to refuse, so she reached out with trembling hands to take the package. It was heavier than expected. As she tore away the paper, he said, "Mom told me your most prized possession is your late mother's Bible, so…"

Unveiling the beautiful box, she saw the cross engraved in the hinged top. "So you made me this to keep Mama's Bible in." Smiling, he nodded. "It's beautiful." Hurrying to the sofa, she sat and placed the box on the coffee table, where a rather battered Bible rested. She opened the lid and dropped the Bible into the box. "Perfect fit. Thank you."

"That's not all you left behind," he said.

"What else?"

He looked her straight in the eye and said, "Me."

Fawn caught her breath and slowly lowered the Bible box to the coffee table. "You?"

"Oh, and this." He dipped two fingers into his shirt pocket and drew out a ring—a diamond ring.

It actually hurt to breathe now, her chest was so tight that it felt as if her heart was trying to beat its way out. "Th-that's Jackie's."

"Not anymore," he said, swiftly crossing the room to park himself on the corner of the coffee table. He bowed his head. "If you'd just given me another week, I could've done this properly, but you ran away and forced my hand."

"Forced your hand?"

"You can't just appear in a guy's life, standing in his kitchen like some vision of perfection, teach him truths he's never heard before, open his heart in ways he never dreamed possible, show him a richer future than he ever imagined for himself and then just disappear. You never even gave me a chance to tell you how much I love you. One kiss and you bolt—"

She nearly knocked him off the coffee table when she threw her arms around him. "Dix!"

"Ah!" He caught her against him, gasping. And then he laughed softly. "That's what I drove five hours for. Don't let go. Don't ever let go."

"Dix! Do you mean it?"

"I'm not going home without you. There is no home without you now."

"I love you!"

"Thank God," he said on a long sigh. "I'd hate to be married to a woman who doesn't love me."

She laughed, tears filling her eyes, and slid back onto the edge of the sofa. "Give me that ring."

"Now, now," he teased, going to one knee, "let's do something the way it's supposed to be done."

Grinning, she gave him her hand. "Fawn," he began, only to frown. "What's your full name?"

"Fawn Michelle Ambor. My great-grandmother was French."

"Lenape, French, Italian and maybe Welsh," he said, grinning. "God must really love me."

"He knew you needed a mostly Lenape woman," she teased.

"Do I ever! Fawn Michelle Ambor," Dixon said, "will you do me the very great honor of marrying me and blessing me with your love for the rest of my life?"

"Yes!"

He slid the ring on her finger and stood,

pulling her up with him for a long, sweet kiss. "My first love," he whispered, hugging her close, "my only love, Merry Christmas."

"Merry ever after," she said. "When can we go home?"

"Looks like a New Year's wedding," Grandmother said cheerfully.

"Guess that means we all have to go," Dawn grumbled.

"Uh, yes, please," Dixon said, smiling at them. "I know Mom would love that." He looked at Fawn then. "Wow. That's at least ninety thousand words a day. You see how much I love you."

Laughing, Fawn pulled him down for another kiss, thanking God that she was the right twin. Together they would make Jackie's last months—years?—as happy as possible, and they'd give Bella a happy home, loving each other with all their might.

First love. Only love.

What better Christmas gift could they have?

* * * * *

*Don't miss these other stories
from Arlene James:*

*THE RANCHER'S HOMECOMING
HER SINGLE DAD HERO
HER COWBOY BOSS*

Available now from Love Inspired!

*Find more great reads at
www.LoveInspired.com*

Dear Reader,

Resentments can color our lives and steal our joy in many ways. Even when hostility and resentment are founded in fact, we often don't know the full story. A young child, such as Dixon was, simply can't understand until the emotional storm is long past, for instance. That's why it's always best to simply forgive and go on. But when the person who hurts us is someone close, that can be so very difficult—unless God intervenes.

Thankfully, God is patient and loves us too much to let us harbor resentment forever. He'll give us opportunities to put our resentments behind us, but we must take them. The harder and longer we resist, the more extreme His measures may become.

Forgiveness brings blessings that we can't imagine while we're sulking in our resentment dungeon. Like Dixon, however, we can find peace and unimagined love through forgiving others.

God bless,

Arlene James

CHRISTMAS EVE COWBOY

Lois Richer

This book is for my own Christmas Eve cowboy.
Happy anniversary!

For God has said, "I will never fail you. I will never abandon you." So we can say with confidence, "The Lord is my helper, so I will have no fear. What can mere people do to me?"
—*Hebrews* 13:5–6

Chapter One

"Mommy, can I have five hundred dollars?"

"What?" Elizabeth Kendall froze in the act of receiving her just-purchased potatoes from the farmers' market seller to stare at her five-year-old daughter. "Why?"

"To buy one of those." Zoey pointed.

Elizabeth turned to look across the town square and locked gazes with the most searching brown eyes she'd ever seen.

Then she caught her breath because this guy also had the heart-stopping good looks of a cowboy actor just departed from the set of an old Western movie. He was tall and lanky, wearing a battered leather jacket with sheepskin lining, jeans and boots. His Stetson was pushed back, exposing his face to the brilliant winter sun. He slouched against a beat-up red truck, cradling a wiggling puppy in his roughened hands. Several more canine babies frolicked in a box on the ground in front of him. Beside them stood a cardboard sign with hand-painted lettering.

Puppies for sale: $50

"That says fifty dollars, sweetie. Not five hundred." Elizabeth knew what was coming. A shiver ran down her spine even though the Montana morning wasn't that cold, at least not for this first day of December. But then her resolve to avoid dogs had nothing to do with the temperature.

"Fifty dollars isn't as much as five hundred dollars, right?" Zoey asked. "So if I can't have my daddy for Christmas, could I have one of those puppies?"

"I'm sorry, sweetheart." The longing in Zoey's green-eyed gaze hit Elizabeth right in the heart yet...*I can't have another dog. I can't go through losing again.*

"You always say no." Zoey glowered at her. "I want that puppy!" she shrieked before racing across the town square toward the cowboy.

Knowing all the busybodies in the little town of Snowflake would soon be gossiping about her and Zoey made Elizabeth pause before following her child. Finally she walked toward the cowboy, tension increasing with each step.

He's not James, her brain reminded her. *He can't hurt you.*

"What kind are your dogs?" Zoey's now uber-friendly tone drew smiles from other shoppers. Elizabeth winced at her daughter's pseudo-innocent look, which meant she was fully aware of the attention. Her kid was a con artist.

"The puppies are a mixture of Lab and springer spaniel." Seeing Zoey's blank look, the hunky cowboy grinned. "They're just plain dogs. Hello."

When he tipped his hat to Elizabeth like they did in the movies she felt an inner flutter. A perfunctory smile lifted his lips but didn't reach his intense gaze. Full of secrets, his eyes reminded her of Belgian chocolate—ordinary-looking until you bit into it. Then you couldn't think of anything else.

"I'm sorry she bothered you." Elizabeth fought back regret as Zoey cuddled one of the animals. "Honey, you have to give it back."

"I want this puppy for Christmas. I'm calling him Mr. Beasley." She giggled as a pink tongue licked her nose. "See, Mommy? He loves me already."

Zoey asked so little. Elizabeth yearned to say yes. But memories wouldn't let her.

"Um, he is a she," the cowboy murmured. "So that would be *Mrs.* Beasley, or actually Ms. Beasley." He caught Elizabeth's eye roll and shrugged. "I'm just saying."

"Whatever." His generous grin weakened her knees. She focused on Zoey. "Honey, you can't have that puppy."

Fury ignited sparks in her daughter's emerald eyes. Elizabeth wondered who among the shoppers would understand why any mom would deny her daughter a puppy.

"This is *my* dog." Zoey cuddled the animal closer, giggling when it burrowed into the sleeve of her soft pink jacket. "He—" she glanced at the cowboy and corrected "—she loves me, even if my daddy doesn't."

"Brett Carlisle, ma'am." The cowboy's voice turned conspiratorial. "May I handle this?"

"We can't have a dog," Elizabeth insisted.

"I understand." He hunkered down next to Zoey. "Listen, kiddo, I don't give my puppies away unless parents okay it."

"Why?" Zoey frowned.

"Because having a puppy is a big responsibility." He glanced at Elizabeth. "Your mom's a doctor, right?"

"Uh-huh." With every second Zoey was bonding more tightly to the puppy, which wasn't the only reason Elizabeth desperately

wanted to get away from this man with mesmerizing eyes and too-cute dogs.

"Everybody calls Mommy Dr. Liz but her
name's really Elizabeth."

"Elizabeth Kendall. And you've met Zoey,"
Elizabeth said.

"Nice to meet you both." Brett nodded and
smiled.

"You, too." Elizabeth shifted impatiently.
Was he going to help or not?

"I can't let you have a puppy unless your
mom says it's okay, Zoey." Brett's voice softened. "Your mom says you can't have this
puppy."

Zoey's chin jutted out, rebellion filling her
freckled face.

"Honey, I have to do more shopping before the market closes." Elizabeth rested her
hand on Zoey's shoulder and nodded at the
cowboy. "Thank you for letting her hold the
puppy."

"You're welcome. Bring her to my ranch.
I have lots of babies she can hold." Brett
grinned at her surprise. "Baby animals. I

rescue and nurture them until they can be taken back to the wild."

"The wild?" Elizabeth arched one eyebrow.

"I rehabilitate baby deer, foxes—wild animals." Brett's rumbly voice held amusement.

"Those two *C's*." Zoey pointed at the logo on his truck. "What do they mean?"

"They stand for the Double C Ranch. My dad's name is Clint Carlisle."

A current raced from his dark eyes straight to Elizabeth's pulse. She didn't want a connection with him or any man. That was why she'd come to Snowflake, because it was light-years away from New York and James and the feeling that she'd never again be whole.

"You and your father ranch together?" Elizabeth guessed.

"We did. Dad's been ill." A glimmer of pain flickered. What wasn't Brett saying?

"I'm sorry." She didn't want to empathize with him but she couldn't help it.

"Thanks. Dad loves the ranch. He's a great

father." Brett ruffled Zoey's strawberry blonde curls. "I'm sure your daddy is, too."

"My daddy doesn't want me." Zoey's too-old tone bit into Elizabeth's heart.

"Sorry." Brett's dismayed gaze dropped to Elizabeth's bare ring finger.

"*I* want my daddy for Christmas but Mommy says I can't have him." Zoey's pathetic tone and meekly lowered head made Elizabeth frown. "So now I want a dog. *This* dog."

"But—" Brett's sideways glance made Elizabeth feel worse for denying her daughter a puppy.

"The other kids at school all have daddies," Zoey murmured into the dog's fur, accompanying the words with a pathetic sigh. "I'm the only one who doesn't."

"That's tough," Brett murmured.

"A puppy would sure help." Zoey peeked at him through her long lashes.

Enough.

"The market closes at noon. We must go."

Who was she kidding? Her daughter wasn't going to release that puppy anytime soon.

"Hey, Pastor Bill." Brett grinned at the approaching rotund minister. "I think Norma's already sold all of those lemon tarts you like so much."

"Norma wouldn't do that to me. How're you doing, Brett?" Pastor Bill clapped him on the shoulder, greeted Zoey and Elizabeth then asked Brett, "How are the sets for the Christmas program coming?"

"Okay." He shrugged. "They're not complicated."

"Vida doesn't do complicated." Pastor Bill scowled. "Unfortunately, she left for Denver this morning to visit her brand-new grandson. Which means we need a new director." His eyes narrowed. "Say, Dr. Liz. I'm on Snowflake's medical board and I seem to recall your résumé included extensive music knowledge. How about leading the Christmas Eve kids' choir?"

"Mommy could." Zoey's excitement made Elizabeth wince. "She sings good."

"Well," Elizabeth said, then shook her head. "I'm sorry, Pastor. Vida asked me last night. I declined." She ignored Zoey's crestfallen face. "I can't."

"This isn't a formal choir, just kids singing on Christmas Eve," the minister countered. "Nothing fancy."

"I'd mess it up. Sorry." She felt guilty for refusing. The memories and James's criticisms wouldn't be silenced.

You always disappoint, Lizzie. She'd hated that denigrating name. *Next time let someone else do it and save yourself embarrassment.*

"Snowflake's kids singing on Christmas Eve is our oldest tradition." Pastor Bill's forehead furrowed. "Seriously reconsider, will you, Dr. Liz?" He waved at the woman beckoning to him. "Guess I better get Norma's tarts before the market closes."

"I need to shop, too. Come on, Zoey." Elizabeth held out her hand.

"I wanna play with the puppy." Zoey's stubborn gaze met hers.

"Let her play while you finish shopping."

Pastor Bill ruffled Zoey's hair. "You can watch her from any place in the square. She'll be safe with Brett. Everybody in Snowflake will vouch for him. He's lived here his whole life."

So refusing would make it seem like she didn't trust either her pastor or Brett.

"Folks'll be real disappointed if we cancel the kids' choir. You being part of Snowflake and with all that musical knowledge..." The pastor's hint was left hanging as he jogged away.

"It can't matter that much," Elizabeth muttered.

"The whole town attends the Christmas Eve kids' choir service. It's tradition." Brett smiled. "Go shop. Leave Zoey with me. Maybe I can dissuade her about the puppy before you come back," he added sotto voce.

More contact with this disturbing man? "I don't want to bother—"

"It's no bother. I love kids, though I'm not around them much."

"You don't have any?" Curiosity built as Brett affectionately studied Zoey.

"Not married." He glanced at his watch then back at her. "Six minutes left. Trust me, Doc."

Elizabeth hadn't trusted anyone since James and look how that had turned out. But Snowflake was a small town, and judging by the number of people who called out greetings, Brett *was* well-known and respected. And she'd be less than sixty feet away.

Zoey wouldn't leave without a protest so she decided to shop first then fight the puppy battle after the stalls closed, when most of the townsfolk would be gone.

"Okay." Elizabeth bent beside Zoey who looked totally infatuated with the puppy. "You can stay here and hold the puppy, but remember—we are *not* taking her home. Got it?"

"Yeah." Zoey pressed a kiss against the dog's fur, her face clearly telegraphing she wouldn't give up without an argument.

Frustrated, Elizabeth hurried toward the

fresh bread stall then glanced back. Brett squatted beside Zoey as the two laughed at the antics of the other puppies.

"They sure look good together." Ida McCloskey handed over Elizabeth's preorder. "Zoey is exactly what Brett needs. He'd never admit it but that man gets real lonely on his daddy's ranch, following his daddy's dream."

"Ranching wasn't Brett's choice?" Elizabeth was intrigued.

"The guy's desperate to be a veterinarian. He was leaving when his dad took sick and—" She shook her head. "Sure you can't lead the kids' choir, Dr. Liz?"

"I can't, Ida." Elizabeth was learning Snowflake had no secrets.

"'I *can* do all things through Christ, who strengthens me,'" Ida quoted and winked. "That's what I keep telling Brett about his veterinarian dream. Now you best get over to Mabel's stall before she gives away your order."

Walking across the square, Elizabeth

couldn't help a second glance at the cowboy. Her heart skipped when Brett pressed back the tangle of strawberry blonde curls that almost reached Zoey's waist. His expression snagged Elizabeth's breath. Why couldn't James have looked at his daughter like that? Why couldn't he have looked at *her* as if she was precious, cherished?

She blushed when Brett caught her staring.

What was it about this cowboy that made Elizabeth think of Christmas wishes and mistletoe kisses?

"Do you like kids?"

Warning! Danger.

Brett tore his gaze from the lovely blond doctor, electrifying in her bright blue jacket to focus on her daughter.

"Who doesn't like kids?" he asked.

"My daddy. Least not me."

Her stark response shocked him. "Who said so?"

"My mommy." Her green eyes swirled with sadness. "She 'splained 'bout him last night 'cause I made a big fuss. But I had to," she wailed. "I found a picture of him and Mommy. I didn't even know I had a daddy!"

Elizabeth was chatting with Mabel Montgomery. From what he'd seen of mom and daughter at church Sunday mornings, Doc seemed devoted to her kid. Why keep Zoey's father a secret?

"Maybe she was protecting you," he mused aloud.

"Like from a bad man?" Zoey frowned. "Mommy said Daddy didn't want us. I dunno why. I musta did sumthin' wrong." A crease pleated her pale forehead. "Only I can't 'member what."

Brett realized this poor kid had the same doubts he'd had years ago when he'd learned his mom had abandoned him and his dad. "You didn't do anything, Zoey."

"How do you know?" Zoey tilted her head, her riot of curls jiggling.

"Kids can't make their parents not love them." Surprised by the fierceness of his urge to hug her, Brett brushed her cheek.

"I dunno." Zoey wrinkled her nose dubiously.

"I know. You never did anything that made your daddy not love you."

"So why doesn't he?" Zoey's plaintive question made Brett scrounge for an answer to soothe her hurting heart.

"Some people just can't love." A picture of Wanda suddenly filled Brett's mind.

She'd claimed to love him yet she'd dumped him without apology. Facing shame, embarrassment and a load of wedding debt she'd accumulated all over town, debt he'd only just paid off, made him avoid romance. For the past two years he'd focused solely on running the ranch.

Until this morning when Elizabeth Kendall and her cute kid reminded you of your loneliness and lost veterinary college dream.

Only it wasn't lost anymore, though he was still lonely.

So what do I do, God?

Brett blinked as a shadow fell over them. "Hey, Grant."

"Hey." His neighbor smiled as he tousled Zoey's mass of curls. "Pretty hair."

"Thank you. I'm Zoey."

"Pleased to meet you, Miss Zoey." Grant gallantly shook her proffered hand. "Brett, the missus says our kids are getting two of your puppies for Christmas. Can you keep 'em till Christmas Eve?"

"Sure. Which ones?" Seeing Zoey clutch her puppy until Grant left, Brett had a hunch fireworks were in the offing. Seeing Elizabeth return he eased the animal from Zoey's clutches and returned it to the box. "Did you get everything?" The way Doc's flaxen hair sparkled in contrast to her jacket mesmerized him.

"More than." The pretty doctor chuckled as she held up bulging bags.

Stay uninvolved. Brett was glad for the interruption of more customers, which left only Zoey's pup and another unsold.

"Good day for puppy sales," Elizabeth said.

"It'll buy more dog food." The shyness Wanda had always mocked overtook him at the inquisitive looks they were getting. "I'd better get home for lunch."

"I'm hungry, too." Zoey picked up her puppy again. "A man said there's going to be food at a roaster. Can we get some, Mommy?"

"A *roaster*?"

"*The* Roaster." Brett chuckled at Elizabeth's confusion. "If you haven't realized, this town is nuts about Christmas. December first, today, marks the kickoff of Snowflake's official Christmas season."

"Ah." A cloud filled her eyes.

"The Roaster is really an excuse to cook hot dogs over a fire in the fairgrounds. The high school band plays carols. Service groups sell coffee, hot chocolate and homemade pie." *What are you, Brett, the Chamber of Commerce?*

"Sounds fun." Dr. Liz's smile destroyed his concentration.

"The fudge booth is my favorite," he blurted.

"What's a fudge booth?" Elizabeth's spiky hairstyle emphasized her prominent cheekbones. Interest twinkled in her hazel eyes.

So Zoey gets her green eyes from her father? And then... *Butt out, Brett.*

"The fudge booth is another Snowflake tradition." Zoey and Elizabeth gaped at him as if he'd lost his marbles. "You have to see it."

"Mommy's car's broken. Can you take us?" Zoey pleaded.

"An oil change," Doc corrected.

"I *could* take you," Brett offered. "The whole town goes. It's—"

"Tradition." Elizabeth's silver-bell laugh made his routine day sparkle with excitement.

"Snowflakers are big on tradition." *What's with your interest in the town's doctor?*

"Snowflakers?" She barely smothered her smile.

"The townsfolk. Us." They all called her Dr. Liz but Elizabeth suited this classy woman better. Doc made *their* relationship seem more personal.

"Meaning we're part of Snowflake now?" Her forehead pleated.

"So you might want to consider leading the kids' choir."

"Not you, too." Something—regret?—flickered across her face.

"Everyone loves the kids' Christmas concert. It's our kickoff to Christmas Day. We all go. You'd be doing us a big service," Brett added quietly.

"I can't." Doc's refusal decided it for him.

Brett was going to break his rule and get involved. For the sake of the town.

He should be heading home to check on his dad and complete a list of ranch work longer than his arm. And yet he couldn't shake the notion that if he showed this fancy doctor and her cute daughter that Snowflake was more than a blot on the landscape, she'd reconsider leading the choir.

"Come with me to The Roaster." Brett watched her eyes flare.

"Um—" Elizabeth hesitated.

"You should learn about where you live." The last thing Brett wanted to do was make Zoey cry but he needed to extricate the puppy. He looked to Elizabeth, who wore the same long-suffering look he'd seen other women wear when they had to break their kids' hearts.

"Zoey," she said quietly.

"I could buy him—her with my 'llowance." The kid's pleading gaze slipped from Brett to her mother. "Please?"

Elizabeth shook her head.

"I want this dog!" Zoey sucked in an angry breath.

Elizabeth's jaw firmed, determination meeting Zoey's iron will.

"I need to tuck her in with her brothers now." Wondering why the kid couldn't have a dog, Brett lifted it from Zoey's clinging fingers. "Come on, Mrs. Beasley."

"You're gonna call her Mrs. Beasley?" Zoey's face beamed. "Mommy, that's my name."

"I know," Doc murmured.

"It suits her." With the animals nestled in blankets, Brett set the box behind his seat in the truck. "Fresh air tires them out. They'll sleep." He turned to Elizabeth. "The Roaster?"

Brett felt like a pimply-faced teen and figured he sounded like it, too. He hadn't asked anyone out since Wanda. *Doc's different.*

"I'll be good, Mommy." Zoey hopped from one foot to the other, curls jiggling.

"Well—*if* you keep your promise, okay." Elizabeth then added, tongue in cheek, "Since it's *tradition*. As Snowflake's newest citizens it's undoubtedly our civic duty."

"Like the choir?" Brett couldn't help it. This could be his last Christmas in Snowflake. He wanted perfect memories. "For the kids?"

"You're persistent but the answer is still no." Doc gave him a look meant to quell. "Let it go?"

"For now." Brett helped them inside his truck and drove off, aware that every eye in the square was on them. The phone lines would be burning up.

Let them talk. Doc's a beautiful woman but I'm not getting involved. I won't be here long enough. That's the plan. Right, God?

Chapter Two

"This is nice of you, Brett." Elizabeth's hazel eyes glinted gold flecks in the afternoon sun. "Snowflake isn't the easiest place to fit in."

"You fit in at church," he said without thinking.

"I've never seen you there." She studied him curiously.

"Dad and I usually sit in the back row."

"You should bring *him* to The Roaster." Doc's furrowed forehead said she was rethinking this...*date*?

Uninvolved, remember?

"Dad wouldn't come," Brett said. "Zoey, how're you doin'?"

"Are we there yet?" That age-old question of kids in a vehicle made Brett chortle.

"Yes." He pulled onto the grassy verge of the street, wondering how to phrase his next comment. "Uh, Doc, this park isn't paved and your shoes..."

"I always wear heels." She glanced at her four-inch spikes. "I need the height."

He let it go. He wasn't going to tell classy Elizabeth, with her fashion-model hair and cover-girl makeup, her probably-cashmere jacket with the handmade angora scarf, her tailored jeans and those fascinating shoes, that she didn't *need* anything.

But when she alighted, only to falter over a hole in the grass, Brett held out his arm. And she took it! Funny how the sun felt warmer.

"What's first?" Zoey gaped at the chaos.

"Coffee." Elizabeth grinned. "And a doughnut?"

Brett couldn't help returning her smile. *Keep your distance* was easier said than done.

"Coffee and doughnuts coming up. Hot chocolate for Zoey?" He grinned when the little girl's eager nod set her curls waggling. So cute. *Stupid father.*

"I want this recipe." Elizabeth licked doughnut glaze from her fingertips.

"Good luck." Brett snickered at her puckered brow. "Bessie Flett started selling doughnuts at The Roaster over seventy years ago. Her progeny now consider making Christmas Roaster doughnuts their civic duty. Her recipe is top-secret."

"Local unspoken rules again." Elizabeth's expression softened as Zoey accepted a bright green balloon with glittery snowflakes on it from a six-foot snowflake. "Snowflake's a great place for families."

"Yep." He liked that she didn't fuss about the breeze messing her hair. "You'd find it easier to fit in if you directed the kids' choir."

"Mabel already hinted that." Elizabeth's tone was droll.

"And?" Brett asked hopefully.

"I'd make a mess of it." She lost the sparkle in her eyes.

"We don't need a qualified choral director, Doc. It's just kids singing." He could look at her all day and not tire.

"Is that the fudge booth?" She pointed to a shanty hauled onto the grounds.

"Yes. The—um, elves—" Brett grimaced "—cook the ingredients in that copper kettle. When it's ready, they pour it on the marble slab to work. Wanna watch?"

"Elves?" Her impish grin mocked him in the nicest way. "Tradition time, Zoey." She stepped forward, caught her heel and grabbed his hand.

While Brett squeezed her fingers, a feeling bloomed inside that had nothing to do with the temperature or her firm grip. Though indefinable, whatever that feeling was, he liked it.

"This town is quite amazing." She forgot to release his hand as she gazed around.

Brett didn't mind, content to hold it and watch her as she studied the fudge-making Fletts in their red pointy hats and green jackets stirring the bubbling mixture in the pot. Zoey was caught up in the antics of the town's mascot but Elizabeth remained riveted by the fudge-making.

Was this what it felt like to have a family? A burst of longing surprised Brett.

"So they sell this fudge?" Elizabeth licked her lips.

"If there's any left." Brett hid his smile. "First they hand some to everyone. Free of charge."

"Really?" Her widened eyes met his. "Glorious food and a whole month of celebration. I don't see how Snowflakers stay slim."

"We work it off the rest of the year." When several people stopped to visit, Brett dropped Doc's hand.

Tomorrow speculation about them would be rife. Well, he'd survived gossip before. At least *she* wouldn't be dumping him at the altar.

"That's quite a gift you have for remembering names," he complimented when they were alone once more.

"How can you help someone if you can't even remember their name? Speaking of—who's the woman selling hand-painted scarves?"

Brett didn't have to look. "Emma Feinstein."

"I'll buy one as a Christmas gift for my office manager. They're gorgeous. What?" she demanded crankily when Brett's grip stopped her. "Don't worry, I won't fall on my face."

"I'm not worried. If you fell you'd just get up again." *Too personal, Brett.* "Your office manager is Emma Feinstein's daughter. She probably already has a couple of those scarves." Realizing he was still holding her arm, he quickly let go.

"That could have been embarrassing." Elizabeth grimaced. "Thanks."

"Mommy," Zoey huffed, her breath forming white clouds as she hopped up and down. "People are dancing."

"Outside? In winter?" Wrinkling her nose in disbelief, Doc said, "Where?"

"Over there." Brett found himself hurried along as Elizabeth eased her way through the crowd until she'd wiggled into a front-row view of couples swaying to "We Wish You a Merry Christmas."

"Dancing in snow boots?"

"Snowflakers love to dance," Brett whispered against her ear. "Want to join them?"

"Dance with you?" Longing flared before she frowned. "I'm not very good."

"It's not a contest. Come on, Doc." He slid his arm around her waist, clasped her hand in his and drew her close. "Snowflake can't have a doctor that doesn't dance," he teased to ease the sudden tension on her face.

"I hope you don't regret this." But she moved fluidly, matching his steps easily as the tempo changed to a faster rhythm, the height of her heels impeding her not a whit.

This could be his last December in Snowflake. Brett had vowed to savor every single celebration. Was that why he so easily abandoned his usual restraint?

Relishing Elizabeth's giggle, he twirled her around a second time, grinning when wisps of her bangs tangled in her lashes and stuck to her damp forehead. Just for a moment Brett wished the music would never stop, that he could let go of his problems and enjoy life. But there was a chance to have his dream.

Taking that chance will hurt Dad.

"Can I dance?" Zoey demanded.

Without missing a beat Elizabeth lifted her hand from his shoulder and linked it with her daughter's. Brett followed suit and their threesome moved over the crisp grass. Zoey's laughter brought smiles to those around them.

If it wasn't for that chance, Brett might reconsider staying in Snowflake.

Because of Elizabeth?

"You must be a popular escort." Half an hour later Elizabeth, flushed and thrilled by their dance, gratefully sipped the coffee Brett brought her. "You're a very good partner."

"So are you."

"I'm not usually," she said, feeling the rush of heat to her cheeks.

"I don't go to many dances since—" Brett gulped, looked uncomfortable.

"Since?" She immediately backtracked. "Sorry. None of my business."

"You'll hear about it, anyway. No secrets in Snowflake." He snickered when she completed the last part with him then sobered. "I was engaged. She walked out before the wedding."

"Right before?" Elizabeth winced when he nodded.

"Ten minutes before the ceremony."

Why would any woman walk away from a gorgeous guy like Brett?

"May I ask what happened?"

"Wanda said she couldn't spend the rest of her life with an uneducated cattleman in a Podunk town nursing an old man. My dad." Brett's voice brimmed with…shame?

"She couldn't have thought that through *before* your wedding day?" Indignant on his behalf, Elizabeth snapped, "Sounds like you're well rid of her."

Brett stared in astonishment.

"I'm sorry if I've offended—"

"You haven't, Doc. It's just that's the first time I've considered her leaving a blessing." Brett's face reddened. "I mean it's taken me ages to pay—"

"She left behind wedding debts?" Disgusted when he nodded, she muttered, "Well rid of her," and was surprised when Brett started laughing.

"You're a fantastic ego booster, Doc. Your patients must love you."

"I hope so. Now what I'd *really* like—" Elizabeth coyly peeked through her lashes "—are a couple of pieces of that fudge." And she'd called Zoey a con artist. "And maybe some to take home?"

"One piece I can handle. The rest waits until everyone's served, but there's always lots. They whip up a couple of batches beforehand." He held out a hand to Zoey. "Come on, kid. Let's go get your mom some fudge."

Delighted, Zoey slid her fingers into his and skipped beside him, chatting merrily about Mrs. Beasley. Elizabeth lost her smile. She was going to have to do something about that puppy. And about these odd feelings Brett aroused. She'd never been able to laugh and tease like this with James. He'd never made her feel pretty or complimented her as Brett just had.

"Today's your lucky day, Doc." Brett's voice broke through her introspection. "As a newcomer to Snowflake, they've gifted you with several pieces." He handed her a little box.

"How wonderful." She debated opening it or saving it for later.

"This is for you to eat now." Smiling as if he'd read her mind, Brett extended a napkin with a piece of shiny dark fudge perched on top. "Your first Snowflake tradition."

"It's good, Mommy." Zoey smacked her chocolate-ringed lips.

With Brett and, Elizabeth suddenly realized, almost half the town watching her, she bit into the fudge. As flavors hit her tongue she closed her eyes and savored the sensations.

"Good?" Brett's anxious question made her smile.

"I'll need more boxes and a new diet." At her words, relieved expressions filled the neighboring townsfolks' faces before heads nodded and the buzz of conversation resumed.

"Did you say that just to appease them?" Brett asked quietly.

"I never lie about chocolate." She pinched a corner off his piece and popped it into her mouth. "Do you want the rest of that?"

"Yes." He ate it. "I have a box for Dad, too."

"Maybe he'll sell it to me," she joked. When had she last felt so carefree?

"Can I go jump in the bouncy house?" Zoey barely waited for Elizabeth's nod before she raced across the space, slid off her shoes and flung herself inside.

"No fear. I admire that." Brett studied Zoey. "Why don't you want her to have a dog? And what's the real reason you won't direct the choir?"

"Long stories," she temporized, set off balance by his question.

"I told you about Wanda." He chuckled at her glower.

"Let us not speak that name again," she said in a mock-threatening voice. Ignoring the second question, she said, "I've a mental block about dogs."

"You're afraid of them?" Surprise darkened Brett's eyes.

"No." Elizabeth hesitated. "Getting another dog—I can't do it."

"You keep saying that." Brett's warm gaze made her relax. "Why?"

"Rex was my dog. My parents gave him to me for Christmas when I was thirteen. Rex was the support I clung to when we moved from one military base to another, the friend

I didn't have to make. He was there when I got married, when my parents were killed overseas, when I had Zoey. Through all the milestones Rex was there."

"And you loved him. So what happened, Doc?"

"James caused Rex's death." Pain resurfaced.

"James being?" Brett asked softly.

"My ex-husband. He was driving drunk and hit my dog." Elizabeth squeezed her eyes closed, willing back the pain, wondering why she was telling this to a stranger yet surprised by how easy it was to talk to Brett.

"When was this?"

"After Zoey was born." She gulped down the sadness. "It's silly but even now I can't fathom another dog taking Rex's place."

"Not silly. Another dog couldn't take Rex's place. He's in your heart." Brett slid his hand over hers and squeezed. "Rex is part of you. But maybe you're mourning more than his death."

"His death was the final nail in ending my

marriage," she admitted. "I can't just replace Rex as if he never mattered."

"After grieving for almost five years, you aren't," he said. "But isn't Rex's legacy to you what you want for Zoey?"

"You must really want to get rid of your puppies." Elizabeth wished she hadn't said it as a pained look flickered across his face.

"I have to do that before the end of the year." Brett glanced at the bouncy house where Zoey jumped. A half-sad, half-amused smile filled his face. "Animals can make a huge difference in a lonely child's life."

"What?" She felt insulted. "Zoey has school, her play group, gymnastics and play dates when I can arrange them..."

"Whoa." Brett tilted up her chin so he could peer into her eyes. "No condemnation here. Everyone in Snowflake knows how devoted you are, Doc."

But as they watched Zoey, Elizabeth realized her daughter didn't engage with any of the other kids. How could a puppy help that?

How did Rex help you? She didn't want to think about Rex.

"I was told you wanted to be a veterinarian. What happened to your dream?"

"I'm working on it." Brett changed the subject. "You said you *couldn't* lead the kids' choir. Why?"

"Again with that choir. Why is it so important to everyone—to you?" Exasperated, Elizabeth glared at him.

"Even I was a kid once, Doc." His wry grin caused a flutter to her breathing.

"Meaning?" Brett's reticent expression reminded Elizabeth of patients who didn't want to reveal something.

"My mom left us when I was young," he said. "I don't remember that, but I remember other things about Christmas. That's when I most noticed how different I was. Other kids made Christmas cookies with their mothers. They bought them special clothes for Christmas, made them special gifts. Dad was a great parent but it wasn't quite the same."

"The choir?" she prompted.

"Was the only place I ever felt like every other kid in town." Brett's voice dropped. "I fit in there because we were all the same, just kids singing about Christmas joy. The Christmas Eve kids' choir brings out joy in everyone."

A wistful expression flickered across his face when a pair of little kids raced around the walking snowflake.

"Our choir director, Mrs. Mac, was fierce about our presentation. It had to be as perfect as we could make it." Brett chuckled at the memory. "She made us feel it was our duty to pour our hearts and souls into the music."

"She sounds like one tough lady." Mesmerized by his animation, Elizabeth waited.

"Absolutely," Brett said softly. "I loved that cranky old woman, never more so than the year she gave me a solo part. It taught me I mattered."

"That's what you want for Snowflake's kids," Elizabeth guessed.

"I want them to feel proud when the whole town shows up on Christmas Eve just to hear *them*, to experience the excitement of standing, buttons about to burst, shivering with the anticipation of Christmas Eve, to have that sense of wonder, hope and delight that makes Christmas like nothing else—*I* want to feel it again."

"Mrs. Mac gave you a great legacy." Elizabeth blinked her misty eyes.

"She taught me Christmas is about giving joy to others." His gaze held hers. "But it's more. Our Christmas Eve service bonds Snowflakers. It's the final event in a month-long celebration that draws us to God, the giver of *The Gift*."

"You're so passionate about the choir." Trying not to sound flippant, she added, "Maybe you should direct it."

"I don't read music. I build sets. But you—" Brett's dark eyes narrowed. "I overheard you singing harmony to that new congregational chorus we tried last Sunday, Doc. I could tell right away that you know music. Zoey's right, you do sing good."

"Thanks, but—"

"We need the choir. We're a small town. We're losing people right and left. Our Christmas traditions were originally intended to draw in tourists looking for a way to celebrate. The choir is for Snowflake. That *we* do for *us.*"

"That's why you build the sets," she mused beginning to understand.

"That's why Mabel is eagerly waiting for you to tell her to create some costumes." He grinned at her surprised expression. "That's why Harry Pinder keeps his lambs groomed—in case you want them for the manger scene. And that's why Pastor Bill keeps polishing his Christmas Eve sermon. Because Snowflake's Christmas kids' choir is the one thing hard times, families moving and losing loved ones can't change."

"I understand, Brett." Though his words added guilt, they couldn't cancel out James's condemnation. "But I can't."

"You've had musical training?" he asked.

"I completed my degree in music," she admitted. "But…I'm not your director." The glint in his eye made her nervous.

"Can't you become one?"

"No." The familiar feelings of self-doubt overwhelmed Elizabeth. "I tried once. It went horribly wrong. I…uh, flop under pressure."

"I don't believe that." He studied her, eyes narrowing. "Someone else said that. Someone who put you down, made you feel valueless." Brett's lips tightened when she nodded. "He was wrong, Doc."

"How do you know?" she whispered.

"I see commitment in the love you shower on Zoey, feel it when you sing in church on Sunday morning." He smiled gently. "You have a lot to give. Don't be afraid because of him."

Elizabeth couldn't break the intensity of Brett's stare. Truthfully? She didn't want to. His words, the way he said them, almost made her reconsider. Maybe…

His phone rang.

"Hey, Dad. What's up?" Brett listened for a moment then frowned. "A heart attack? I'll call the ambulance and head home."

"Your father's having a heart attack?" Elizabeth slid into medical mode. "I'll go with you. Zoey, come quick. We have to leave."

Without argument the little girl left the bouncy house and slipped on her shoes while Brett called the ambulance.

"Somebody's having a baby?" she guessed.

"Not quite." Elizabeth smiled at her. "Brett's father is sick. We're going to see him."

"I'm ready." Zoey nodded.

"Let's go." Elizabeth frowned when Brett seemed to move too slowly. "Well?"

"Uh, you should know—"

"We'll discuss it on the way." She slid her hand into his arm. "Fast walk to the truck then a quick stop at my place to get my medical bag."

He nodded. It took only a few moments to retrieve her bag before they left town.

"Is this his first heart attack?"

"It probably isn't a heart attack," he confessed.

"What then?" Elizabeth frowned when he hesitated. "I'll need information to help him."

"It's likely a panic attack. Dad gets them a lot since his stroke several years ago." Brett's embarrassment touched her. "Being alone too long upsets him. I should have gone straight home."

"You're saying he's faking a heart attack?" She wrinkled her nose. "People usually don't fake heart attacks."

"He's not faking. When he can't catch his breath…" Brett's confusion touched her.

"I'll check him out when we get there," Elizabeth assured him. "How long till the ambulance arrives?"

"Twenty-minute wait."

"Good thing I'm going, then." At least James had never criticized her medical ability.

"Thanks, Doc." But something in Brett's tone said he was troubled about her visit to the ranch.

Elizabeth asked several more pertinent questions, mentally preparing her treatment plan as they drove over stubble-covered hills with stands of green pines clustered here and there, boughs sagging as they caught gently drifting snowflakes.

Funny how eagerly she anticipated visiting Brett's ranch.

Chapter Three

"It's lovely." Elizabeth's rapt face reassured Brett as he drove toward the log house that had been home for as long as he could remember.

"Like a snow globe, right, Mommy?" Zoey said.

"Exactly." Doc grasped her medical bag in one hand, her other on the door lever signaling her impatience as he navigated the circular driveway. The moment he braked she was out of the truck and racing toward the house, unimpeded by her high heels.

"Wait!" Knowing he'd need to prepare his father, Brett hurriedly lifted Zoey out and ushered her toward the door. Clint Carlisle wasn't one to filter his irritation.

Inside, Elizabeth had already knelt in front of his dad. One hand rested on his wrist, her stethoscope dangling around her neck. Her coat lay in a careless puddle on the floor. Brett picked it up, stroking one hand down the fabric while she took command.

"Pulse is good. Heart beat steady. Breathe in," she commanded, slipping the stethoscope into her ears. When her patient didn't immediately obey, she repeated more firmly, "Breathe in."

Realizing he was still holding her coat, Brett glanced at the label before hanging it on a hook near the door. Yep, cashmere. Well, Doc was a cashmere kind of lady, something entirely foreign to him and the Double C.

"Dad, this is Dr. Elizabeth Kendall and her daughter, Zoey. Doc heard me on the phone with you and thought she could help."

"Shh. Mommy needs to listen." Zoey held a finger to her lips as Clint opened his lips to protest.

Silence reigned for about fifty seconds before Clint exploded.

"I have my own doctor, missy. I'll call him if I need a checkup." He tugged his shirt closed, roughly dislodging Elizabeth's hand. She appeared unfazed. "What kind of doctor butts in on a guy when he's sleeping?"

"One who's concerned for the health of a man who said he was having a heart attack, though I do prefer treating kids." She calmly tucked her tools into her bag and rose.

Clint glared at her, dark eyes glowering before turning on Brett, his face furious.

"You brought me a *baby* doctor?" he exploded.

Brett exhaled. *It's downhill from here, Lord.*

Except that Zoey intervened. Her coat, like her mother's, sank to the floor as she marched across the room in red-and-green-striped socks. Hands on her hips she glared at Clint.

"My mommy is a very good doctor. She always helps sick people, even cranky ones like you." Her green eyes shot sparks. "You should say thank-you instead of yelling at her. We were at The Roaster an' we danced an' I was playin' in the bouncy castle an' havin' fun till we had to leave to come an' help you."

"I don't need help— The Roaster, huh?" Clint's eyes widened as a curious smile filled his face. "My son danced?" He smirked as Zoey nodded. "Well, well."

Brett almost groaned aloud at the innuendo.

"Did you taste the fudge, little girl?"

"I'm Zoey Kendall, an' the fudge was really good." Curly head tipped to one side she asked in a pity-filled voice, "Couldn't you come 'cause you're sick? Or 'cause you're too old?"

"I am not sick or too old!" Clint's glare returned. "I didn't want to be around all those people. They get silly about Christmas."

"Christmas is Baby Jesus's birthday. That makes people happy not silly." Zoey flopped onto the sofa beside him. "Is your 'tack gone?"

"My what?" His father raised an eyebrow and looked to Brett, who glanced at the doctor.

"Attack," Elizabeth supplied. "As in heart attack. How are you feeling now, Mr. Carlisle?"

"As good as I did when I got up this morning." Clint sniffed in disgust. "Doctors."

Brett wished he could melt like a snowman.

"Make coffee, son," his father ordered. "I need it."

"Tea would be better," Doc said. "Herbal, without caffeine."

Brett admired Elizabeth's pluck in returning his father's glare. The lady brimmed with internal strength, yet she thought she was a flop?

"No stimulants until we make sure you're okay," she ordered.

"I'm fine," his father snarled.

"You told Brett you were having a heart attack." Unfazed, she held his gaze. "The ambulance will have a monitor to check your heart rate more thoroughly."

"I told you not to call the ambulance," Clint roared at Brett.

"Calm down." Elizabeth's command silenced Clint mid-rant.

No weak, ineffectual woman could shut down his father with two words. Brett smiled as he put the kettle on to boil. Doc was going to do the choir. She wouldn't be able to help herself. Zoey tugged on his shirtsleeve.

"Don't the puppies need to eat?" She sounded worried.

"Yes, they do. Thank you for reminding me. I'll go get them." He hurried to his truck, retrieved the box of now-protesting dogs and returned to place them in a little pen he'd built in the corner. "Want to help me get their lunch?"

"Yes." Zoey followed his directions exactly then set the dishes in the pen. "Look at Mrs. Beasley eat."

"Who?" Clint demanded.

"Mrs. Beasley. She's going to be my Christmas gift." Ignoring her mother's muffled "No!" Zoey sat beside Clint. "Where's your Christmas tree?"

"Don't have one, don't want one," Clint snapped.

Elizabeth's gaze locked with Brett's, smiling at Zoey's disbelief. At least Doc wasn't worried about his cranky father's effect on her kid.

"Mister, you gotta have a Christmas tree!" Zoey peered upward. "An' a big one 'cause this house is high."

"Christmas trees make a mess," Clint said as if that was the end of it.

"Everything does." Zoey shrugged. "But messes don't matter at Christmas. When do we get our Christmas tree, Mommy?"

"Maybe next week," Doc answered.

"We're havin' a real Christmas tree this year," Zoey told Clint, eyes sparkling. "Mommy promised."

"If we can find one," Elizabeth added.

"A *good* doctor might have noticed Snowflake is chock-full of trees," Clint sniped.

"So's the Double C. Acres of 'em." Brett ignored his dad's huff. "We could get one for you at the same time as we get ours, Doc.

If there's enough snow maybe we'd take the sleigh. Dad made it. It's fun to ride in with the horses pulling."

"Horses?" Zoey's eyes widened. "Can we, Mommy?" she begged.

"That's very kind, Brett. We'll have to see." Zoey sighed before returning to the dog pen. Elizabeth's troubled gaze followed. Then Doc was the one sighing as her daughter lifted her puppy and carried it to the sofa, where she flopped down next to Clint.

"Do you want to hold Mrs. Beasley?" Zoey asked.

"No." But Clint's gruff tone softened as Zoey lifted the puppy against her cheek. "Why do you call her that?"

"'Cause that's her name." Zoey snuggled the dog in her lap. "Mommy's dog was Rex. Do you have a dog?"

"Had one when I was your age." Clint smiled at some distant memory. The kettle whistled, so Brett made peppermint tea while his father reminisced. "Scout went everywhere with me. Even to school."

"Teachers 'lowed a dog at school?" Her green eyes expanded. "Maybe—"

"I don't think they allow that anymore," Brett intervened, catching Elizabeth's look of dismay.

"Where's your dog now?" Zoey asked.

"Don't have one." Clint's voice hardened. "Not anymore."

"Why not? You gots lots of puppies. Least you did before they got buyed." She frowned at Mrs. Beasley. "She's mine but maybe Brett will let you have one of the other puppies. They need somebody to love 'em. You loved Scout. Didn't you?"

"Yeah." Clint's face grew luminous as he peered into his past.

Just as Brett began pouring tea the ambulance drove up. Following Elizabeth's bidding the attendants strapped Clint to their monitor, which showed no evidence of heart irregularity. After a more thorough examination and a quick consultation with Elizabeth, the conclusion was that Clint Carlisle seemed fit. They departed after a radio appeal to another call.

"I should leave, too," Elizabeth murmured.

"If I have to drink that stuff he made, so do you," Clint snapped.

"Well, thank you. I'd like to stay for tea." With a completely straight face, Elizabeth accepted a cup from Brett, who smothered his grin. Doc was good for his dad. She sampled her tea then asked, "What do you do with your days, Clint?"

"I'm retired. Brett handles the ranch." Clint gulped his tea. His face screwed into a frown, then he smacked the cup on the table.

"Hey!" Zoey glared at him. "You scared Mrs. Beasley." She snuggled the dog close then placed it on Clint's knee before retrieving another mewling pup. "You can hold this one," she said, exchanging it for Mrs. Beasley.

Clint seemed dumbfounded. "You're bossy."

"I'm just helpin'." She snuggled her puppy.

"Would you like tea, Zoey?" Brett loved this child and her temerity.

"May I?" She glanced at her mom, who nodded. "Yes, please."

He poured a few drops into a tiny china cup that had sat in the cupboard for as long as he could remember then added milk until it was almost full. "Here you are."

"Thank you." Zoey's baby finger stuck out as she took a delicate sip then smiled. "It's delicious."

That smile caught Brett's heart and hung on. This warm, bubbly feeling inside must be what it was like to have your own kids. He wished...

"That minister fellow called here a while ago. He's emailing something about that Christmas program." Clint frowned. "Haven't you got enough to do?"

"More than." Brett ignored his father's irritable expression. "But I promised I'd help out. They're shorthanded."

"Mary Parker never needed help with the kids' choir," Clint snapped. "And she did it for ten years."

"So why doesn't she do it this year?" Elizabeth blinked at the sudden stark silence.

"Mary and her family were killed in a car accident last summer." Brett hadn't wanted to tell her. Not yet. "Vida was the only one who'd take it on and she had to leave, so…" He deliberately didn't finish.

"Why don't you do it?" Clint's sarcastic tone and glare would have quelled most women. Doc wasn't most women.

"Mommy has a *magnifience* voice," Zoey offered in a very adult tone.

"Magnificent," Brett corrected, covering his amusement as Doc's cheeks flushed a lovely crimson.

"If my mommy wasn't a doctor, she'd be a singer, right, Mommy?"

"If—maybe." Elizabeth suddenly looked sad.

"If ifs and buts were candy and nuts, we'd all have a Merry Christmas," Zoey recited then returned to sipping her tea.

Clint's burst of laughter echoed to the rafters. "You're a funny kid, Zoey." Admiration filled his father's voice.

Brett bit his lip. For the first time in eons his dad's focus wasn't on himself. Was this little girl with her unabashed spirit the answer to his prayers?

Or was that answer Zoey's mom?

Elizabeth Kendall was certainly an answer to someone's prayers. But not Brett's. Expensively elegant and sophisticated, the lovely doctor would have nothing in common with a rough rancher.

Nothing at all.

Which sure was a pity, even though Brett didn't intend to be a rancher for much longer.

Since she'd met him Elizabeth had struggled to get Brett Carlisle off her mind. Despite extended hours during a minor flu epidemic at the nursing home, drawing up a strict treatment plan for a high-risk pregnancy of twins for a forty-two-year-old mother who refused to let anyone but Elizabeth treat her and arranging an emergency life flight for an injured employee from a nearby ski hill, she failed.

The cowboy wouldn't be dismissed.

Finally she decided to direct the children's Christmas choir. It wasn't because she was bored. It had to do with the town's loss of a director and Snowflake's sense of community.

But mostly she'd decided to do it because of Brett's faith in her. *Someone else told you that. Someone who put you down and made you feel valueless. He was wrong, Doc.*

Was James wrong? Elizabeth desperately wanted to prove he was and thereby forever be rid of the legacy of her ex-husband's denigrating remarks, which still had the power to make her feel useless, unworthy, unacceptable. And she also wanted to do it for that young Brett who'd found himself because of a caring choir director. Most of all Elizabeth clung to the hope that once more directing a choir would forever silence her own inner voices of ineptitude.

"Pastor Bill says you're directing the

Christmas program, Doc. Congratulations. You'll be amazing." Brett slammed his truck door shut and offered his arm to help her navigate the slippery church parking lot. "We've had a foot of snow this week. Don't you have any boots?"

"These are my boots." She pulled up a pant leg to show him the knee-high boots she'd ordered from Pete's Five and Dime. "They're not exactly as described."

"Very nice. Gutsy and easy to look at. Like you." His voice sounded squeaky. Since he seemed in a rush to get her across the parking lot, Elizabeth didn't have time to puzzle out why.

"Thank you." She drew her arm from his when they reached the foyer, half wishing he hadn't hurried their few moments together.

"Where's Zoey?" He glanced behind her as if he expected her daughter to pop out.

"She came earlier with Mrs. House. She looks after Zoey for me." Elizabeth undid her jacket. She caught her breath when Brett's hand rested fleetingly on her shoulder before he slid it off. Had he noticed his effect on her? "Thank you again."

"Welcome." His attention focused on her coat. "Is this lambskin?"

"I think so." She frowned. "Why?"

"I sell wool from my Merino sheep to a place in Billings. They make stuff out of it, mostly mitts and scarves. I wonder if they ever thought of making coats like this?" He hung it up carefully then studied her. "You look lovely," he said quietly. "You always do. Elegant and beautiful."

"Elegant in jeans and a sweater?" She glanced at herself then shrugged. "Thank you for the third time." As the racket of rowdy children in the gathering room penetrated she made a face. "I hope I don't mess this up. About fifty people have told me that this Christmas Eve thing is a huge deal. I don't even know what we're performing."

"You haven't checked over Vida's plan?" Brett's concerned look initiated a tidal wave of worry.

"I haven't had time. The pastor left the material here but I was tied up with a case most of last night, so I couldn't get it." Her determination wavered. "Don't you think I can do it?"

"Of course you can do it. Everybody knows Handel's *Messiah*. Even a hick like me." Brett grinned at her as if it was a sure thing but Elizabeth's breath caught in her throat as she stared at him in horror.

"You're telling me Vida intended for these kids to sing the *Messiah*?" she squeaked, aghast.

"Not all of it," he assured her. "Just parts."

Because that was so much easier. "Which *parts*?" she whispered.

"Uh, the Hallelujah chorus and a couple of other bits. Simple stuff."

Simple? Handel? Elizabeth gulped.

"You'll be great, Doc." Brett reached out and squeezed her arm. "Excuse me now. I have to check out what Ernie's doing with the stable setup we're building. Hope he's not using the table saw or we might need you professionally." He winked. "Just teasing."

Elizabeth watched him leave, feeling as if her lifeboat went with him and she was stranded on a barren island where Handel played in a fog. She found her way to a pew and sank onto it.

Lord, I came to Snowflake to change and grow, to learn to trust You to help me be the person You want. But...the Messiah? *For kids? In less than a month?*

What was she thinking?

I am the Lord, the God of every person on the earth. Nothing is impossible for Me.

The verse from Jeremiah echoed in her head. She'd read it every day this week to instill God's word in her heart. This message was trust Him to do as He promised.

Elizabeth struggled with trusting God, with leaving James and the past behind. James's criticisms were the reason she'd quit singing, quit playing, quit everything to do with her beloved music after that last Christmas fiasco. She wanted to quit now, too, but if she did how could she face Brett?

Elizabeth rose slowly. She wouldn't have

to quit. After tonight Brett and the pastor would be desperate to find someone else to lead the kids' choir.

Funny how thoughts of Brett made her heart race.

"Doc?" Suddenly there he was, standing in front of her.

Elizabeth's heart went skittering. "Did you come back to help me?"

"Uh, no. I just answered the phone and need to pass on a message." His expression said it wasn't a happy message.

She held her breath.

"Ms. Purvis, the church pianist? She fell on ice coming out of her house." Avoiding her gaze he hurried on. "Apparently she's broken her wrist. She won't be playing tonight."

"Or anytime soon. Who's her substitute?" The answer spread across the rancher's sun-tanned face. "There is no pianist," she guessed.

"Remember one thing, Doc." Brett threw an arm around her shoulders and led her toward the kids.

"What's that?" Why did the weight of his arm comfort her?

"Nothing's impossible for God." His arm tightened in a squeeze then let go.

"Right. You don't by chance play piano, do you?"

"Sorry." Brett shook his head. "I'm a cowboy, which means I *can* play the guitar, though not well and mostly by ear. But you can do this, Doc."

Elizabeth figured his encouraging grin could sustain her for…oh, maybe a minute. About as long as it would take before everybody in Snowflake found out that their newest doctor was a failure.

Why had she let Brett's hunky rancher's charm sweet-talk her into this?

Chapter Four

Tuesday afternoon Brett arrived at church well before practice time hoping for exactly this—an encounter with the town's loveliest doctor.

What he hadn't expected was a private performance. For the past half hour he'd sat astounded as Elizabeth brought Handel's music alive. She played beautifully, though Brett knew, because the music had been his dad's favorite since he was a kid, that she skipped some parts.

He clapped effusively when she finished.

Elizabeth leaned over to switch off a machine on the floor beside her. "Hi."

"You recorded that?" Brett figured he'd never tire of the way her silver gilt hair framed her face and those gentle forest-toned eyes. Her dark green turtleneck perfectly mirrored her irises.

"The kids need music to know where to come in. So I made a recording." She leaned to stretch her back. "I hope it works because the last practice was a disaster."

"The first one always is. I've been praying for you and the kids," he said quietly.

"Thank you, Brett. All prayers appreciated." She rose and gathered her things, pink tingeing her cheeks. "I better prepare."

"You'll do a wonderful job." Not sure why he knew that, Brett had an inner certainty that Elizabeth never gave less than her best to anything. "I'll be working in the back hall. Call me if I can help."

"Thank you." She began laying out her music on the choir director's stand while the kids took their places. "Today we're going to try three songs with music," she told them.

Turning a bit, she noted him still standing there and offered a wobbly smile.

Brett gave a thumbs-up. He left the sanctuary, stopped just beyond to listen, then winced before finding Ernie. Later the pastor joined them and turned on a speaker that transmitted the sounds from the sanctuary so they could hear.

"The kids are better, aren't they?" Brett said cheerfully.

"Than what?" Pastor Bill frowned.

"Maybe the music's too hard." He heard Elizabeth call a break.

"We need faith and prayer." A furrow of concern lined the pastor's forehead.

Brett followed the scent of fresh coffee to the kitchen, where Elizabeth sat staring at a wall, her face grim.

"Hey, Doc. Your kids are doing great."

"Forget it, Brett." She looked defeated. "The music is glorious. But adult choirs practice Handel for months. I don't see how Vida expected these kids to master it in a few weeks."

She sounded so…defeated. His heart ached for her. He'd pressured her to do this. *God? Can You help us?*

"What will you do?"

"I don't know. Some of Vida's choices don't fit a children's choir. The annunciation part is very technical but it's such a big part of the Christmas story that I can't cut it." She frowned at him. "I warned you I'd mess this up."

"You're not messing up. We're problem-solving." He silently prayed for ideas. "What if someone recited parts interspersed by a few select choir numbers?"

"It would be a much shorter concert than Vida planned." Her smile faded. "I wouldn't know who to ask."

"I would." He chuckled at her surprise. "When I was a kid Dad sang every note of the *Messiah* every year." Brett exhaled. "The difficulty will be persuading him to help."

Was it stupid to propose Clint? Maybe, but Brett suggested it for the kids. Okay, for Doc, too. Because he wanted her to succeed and he wanted his last Christmas here to be filled with memories he could treasure. Once he left Snowflake, there was no guarantee he'd ever live here again. He needed memories of the life he'd give up.

"Your dad?" Elizabeth studied him then sifted through her music. Snatching his pen she began scribbling on the back of a bulletin. When she lifted her head, her big eyes met his in a flare of hope. "It might work."

"You'll make it work, Doc." Seeing Ernie waiting in the doorway, Brett finished his coffee then retrieved his pen. "Gotta go."

"What are you building?"

"The backdrop of a stable. Vida wanted it." He double-checked. "Will you?"

"I'm not exactly sure what we'll need, but if this choir happens, a stable will certainly be part of it." She smiled. "Brett?"

"Yes?" He rose, soaking in her beauty.

"Keep praying, will you?" she whispered. "I'm not sure I'm up to this."

"You are, Elizabeth," he assured her in a

low voice. "You're strong. As a doctor and a single mother you've had to be. But also, you're a child of God. You are more than a conqueror in Christ."

Brett returned to his work in a prayerful attitude. He had an inner certainty that Doc would succeed. What he wasn't sure of was his dad's cooperation, especially after he learned that Brett wanted to accept the offer of a scholarship to veterinary college. What stopped him was thinking about what his departure would do to Clint and the ranch.

"I need Your leading," he silently begged.

It was the first time since Wanda had walked out that Brett had straight up asked God for something for himself. He wanted to grab his chance at college. Becoming a veterinarian was his dream. But right now he had to focus on helping Doc succeed because he sensed she needed this accomplishment to erase the past.

Funny how important Doc's success was becoming to him. Almost as important as finally achieving his own dream.

* * *

"Are we going to Brett's house so I can see Mrs. Beasley?" Zoey asked from the back seat the following evening.

"You can *visit* her but I have another reason for going." To Elizabeth's dismay Mrs. Beasley was all Zoey talked about. "Be on your best behavior."

"I promise. Do you think Brett and his daddy will like our cookies?"

"I'm sure they will." As she pulled into the ranch yard lit only by a light on a pole Elizabeth thought how a few Christmas lights would enhance the log house. She inhaled for courage as her vocal coach had taught her years ago then realized Zoey was already heading for the house. "Wait!"

Too late. Her daughter was being welcomed inside by the tall, lean cowboy who constantly occupied Elizabeth's brain. Why did Brett fascinate her so?

"Zoey and I brought some Christmas cookies to share." Quashing her silly delight at seeing Brett again, she stepped inside and smiled at Clint, who lay sprawled across the sofa. "And to ask for *your* help."

Okay, God. This is me trusting You.

"With what?" Clint glowered at her suspiciously. His expression softened when Zoey plopped down beside him, Mrs. Beasley on her lap.

"With the Christmas choir." Brett's nod gave her courage. Elizabeth spread her plan on the coffee table in front of his dad. "The only way I can think of to make the kids' choir work is if you help me."

She ignored his spluttering and launched into her plan, begging, pleading and finally using guilt as a motivator. But Clint's stubborn expression and Brett's pursed lips showed her appeal wasn't working.

Feeling like a failure, Elizabeth finally closed the folder and rose.

"Then this Christmas pageant will be a write-off, Clint Carlisle. Because of you."

He straightened, his expression thunderous. Oddly enough Brett smiled and tucked his chin into his chest, hands folded in his lap. What in the—

"Me?" Clint burst to his feet, eyes glinting. "I suppose you'll blab that all over town and then we'll have a repeat of the gossip we endured the last time a woman came here!"

Wanda. Elizabeth detested the comparison.

"I would never gossip about you or anyone else," she promised. "Though I did mention to the pastor that I was going to ask you to help the children."

Brett nodded in a way Elizabeth assumed meant *keep going*. She noticed his twitching lips just before he put his hand over his mouth and gave a feeble cough.

"Pastor Bill will spread it—" Clint stopped when the phone rang. He frowned when Brett handed the receiver to him. "Who's this?... Well, Bill, I don't know who told you that... Of course I know the *Messiah* but... Yes, but... But...I have to go!"

Seconds later a second caller was dismissed just as abruptly. And then a third. Clint's face was beet-red.

"All over town," he snarled, slamming down the phone.

"Mommy says you shouldn't talk to people on the phone when you're mad." Zoey looked up from the puppy, her face puzzled. "Why are you mad, CC?"

"CC?" Clint stared at her. "Why do you call me that?"

"'Cause that's what's on your truck. Isn't it your name?" When he didn't answer, Zoey shrugged.

Brett's hand completely covered his face now, except for those expressive chocolate eyes, which studied Elizabeth with admiration or...?

"I think you should help my mommy make Christmas nice for everybody in Snowflake." Zoey's voice broke the room's tension.

"Oh, you do." Clint toned down his annoyance as he faced Zoey. "Why?"

"'Cause Christmas is a happy time but sometimes people don't feel happy so it's other people's job to help them get happy." She shrugged, her curls shimmering in the light of the flickering fire. "That's what Mrs. Beasley does for me."

Her sweet words and the tender kiss she pressed against the puppy's nose made Elizabeth wince. That puppy was a problem. She glanced at Brett then wished she hadn't because his gaze sent an electric current rippling up her spine.

"I'm not Mrs. Beasley," Clint snapped.

"A course not," Zoey giggled. "You're too big. But you got lots of things to be happy about and some people gots none. So you should help Mommy."

The old man raked a hand through his hair but didn't refuse. Maybe her child's convoluted reasoning would thaw the elder rancher?

"If you did the readings, Dad, you could be behind the stage or in the shadows," Brett suggested. "In fact, that might force everyone to really listen to the words."

"How many songs?" Clint asked.

"Four, maybe five. We need an opening reading to set the stage, one between each song and one to close at the end." Elizabeth held her breath when Clint didn't immediately reject the idea. *You can do all things, Lord. Even soften his heart.*

"Who chooses the readings?"

"You do, but they must fit the songs we'll perform. I feel these selections are easiest for the children." Elizabeth held out the sheet music.

He barely glanced through them. "Who's doing the 'I Know that My Redeemer Liveth' solo?"

Elizabeth gulped. The song she'd flubbed— and to quote James, she'd performed *shamefully.*

"I thought you could read that," she said hesitantly.

"My son tells me you have a beautiful voice. You should sing." Clint's glare penetrated.

"I'm already directing," she said quickly. "And playing."

"I'm already recuperating from a stroke. Could relapse anytime." He leaned back against the sofa, a smile flickering at the corner of his mouth. "Don't know if I should take on all that stress."

"You're not—"

"I'll help if you sing. Take it or leave it." Clint looked as if he'd just scored a goal.

"But I haven't sung in eons." Turning to Brett for support she received only an encouraging smile. "That solo isn't the easiest to perform."

"So practice," Clint said.

"We don't have a pianist." Elizabeth glanced from father to son. "You expect me to play, direct and sing?"

"We'll use the church's sound system to record the music ahead of time." Brett's cheerful voice irritated her. Elizabeth grasped at straws.

"We still need something else in the program. Four or five songs and a few readings will be too short." *Solve that*, she fumed silently.

"Congregational singing of carols helps

spread the Christmas spirit." Clint's gloating tone bugged her.

"Not enough." Elizabeth watched the two men exchange a glance.

Clint frowned. Brett offered, "The high school band?"

"To go with the *Messiah*?" Elizabeth sighed in defeat. "There's another thing. An expectant patient is due Christmas Eve. Her other three kids have arrived right on her due date. If the town's only obstetrician isn't back from his Hawaiian vacation I'll be called to deliver. What if she goes into labor in the middle of the concert?"

"Doc Terry can come out of retirement for that. Or we'll have an intermission." Clint leaned forward. "Let me see those songs again so I can figure out the readings. I need a few days to put something together."

"I need months," Elizabeth said gloomily.

"I think you'll both pull it off without a snag," Brett proclaimed with a grin. "Now, can we sample some of those cookies you brought, Zoey?"

"Wait a minute, what are *you* contributing to this?" Clint demanded.

"Yes, what?" Elizabeth pinned Brett with her most severe look.

"Building the sets," he said quickly.

"Refurbishing former sets, actually." Clint frowned at Elizabeth. "What else do you need help with?"

"I thought maybe the kids could play bells or something for one of the songs. Only I can't find any." She frowned at Brett, who was shifting uncomfortably. "Any ideas?"

"About bells?" He blinked, nonplussed. "Where would I find bells?"

"I don't have a clue." Elizabeth crossed her arms. "But you know what? You conned me into doing this and I've got my hands full so I'm going to leave finding bells up to you while I keep Mabel from stitching up a bunch of angel costumes for the kids."

"What's wrong with angel costumes?" Clint demanded.

"Her idea is way over the top, besides

which the kids do not in the least resemble angels when they sing." She glared at him.

"But they will, Doc." Brett grinned and put the kettle on. "We have faith in you."

Which would make it even more embarrassing when the evening was a colossal flop, Elizabeth thought gloomily while watching Zoey and the men dip shortbread cookies into the tea Brett poured. She felt exhausted, but at least Clint would help.

"When do we get our Christmas tree from your ranch?" Zoey demanded.

"Not yet, sweetie," Elizabeth said to shush her. Their lives were getting entirely too entwined with Brett and Clint Carlisle.

"Teacher said it's three weeks till Christmas. That's not hardly any time." Zoey snuggled Mrs. Beasley on her lap, her face troubled. "Is your sleigh ready, CC?"

"Zoey!" Elizabeth winced at the loudness of her voice. "We're not going to trouble these men to get us a tree. Now finish your tea. We have to leave."

"Just so happens I looked at that sleigh two nights ago, Zoey," Clint said.

Elizabeth saw Brett's eyes widen as he gaped at his father.

"Made me decide I'd check out the forest in the back forty Saturday evening. Want to come?" Clint winked at Zoey, who immediately whooped for joy.

"Uh, Dad—"

"Can we, Mommy?" Zoey's eyes gleamed. "I never rided in a sleigh before. Can Mrs. Beasley come, too, CC?"

"She's too young." Brett's face was thunderous. "Dad, I—"

"Supposed to snow." Clint smiled at Zoey as if they were coconspirators. "We'll take along some hot chocolate and sing carols."

"Oh, goody!" Zoey jiggled in her chair until she realized her puppy didn't like it.

Truth to tell it sounded like fun to Elizabeth, too, but it seemed Brett didn't want them to go. Why?

"For a man who didn't want to celebrate

Christmas let alone get a tree, you're suddenly very gung-ho," he complained.

"Zoey brings out my Christmas spirit." Clint winked at her, his grin spreading when Zoey grinned back. "About time we made some new memories," he said firmly.

Over the next hour Clint regaled Zoey with stories about his childhood. Her giggles and his laughter made the house hum with joy. Brett pretended to join in, strumming his guitar while Clint and Zoey sang familiar carols, but his mind seemed to be on something else, something that heightened the worried look in his eyes every time he studied his father.

Elizabeth drove home with Clint's invitation for a sleigh ride hunt for a Christmas tree ringing in her ears, but with Brett's dark-eyed anxiety on her mind.

She'd been so busy trying to get help for the Christmas choir she hadn't given a thought to anyone else's troubles. Soon she'd find out if she'd asked too much of Brett.

And pray she hadn't because without him

there to encourage and support her, doubts about failing another choir would over-whelm her.

Chapter Five

To Brett's ear, Saturday morning's choir practice sounded slightly less chaotic than previous ones. He figured it was probably due to the little "talk" Doc had given the kids about their responsibility to make Christmas Eve special for everyone.

Not that they sounded great. But better. Sort of.

"Hi." Doc stood in the doorway of the gym where he was polishing the wooden cradle where Baby Jesus would lie.

"Hi, yourself." To Brett, Elizabeth always looked gorgeous, but today her cherry-red sweater was both appropriate and functional given the cooler weather and the season. "It's too cold for a sleigh ride today, right?"

"Really?" She frowned. "I thought Clint's suggestion of going this afternoon instead of tonight is smart given the expected temperature dip. Zoey and I have our stuff all ready."

"Oh. Good." Part of him danced with joy at the prospect of an afternoon with this special woman. The other part knew an outing together would only make things more difficult later.

Don't get involved, Brett. Too late.

"I'll be finished here in five minutes."

"How's the bell search coming?" She wrinkled her nose at Ernie's drawing of a camel.

"Working on it." Brett gave up polishing. He couldn't concentrate, anyway.

"Something's bothering you." Concern darkened her eyes to a deep forest green. "Would you rather cancel our sleigh ride?"

"You're welcome to come." She *had* to come. "Dad wants to go," he added lamely.

"Then what's the problem?" She tilted her head to one side.

"It's a long story." Brett didn't want to dump his problems all over Doc, though the prospect of sharing appealed. "You're busy."

"Not today. Zoey's gone home with Mrs. House. I'm not on call. I have time." She sat down beside him. "Tell me."

Brett debated but he needed advice and she wasn't a gossip so he finally gave in.

"For a long time I've wanted to be a veterinarian," he began. "I planned to attend college after high school."

"I heard." Elizabeth nodded, hair wildly askew.

He hid his grin, knowing she'd raked her fingers through the silver strands during practice. She took the choir so seriously, as if any failure would show a flaw in her. He didn't get why.

"You canceled your plans when your dad had a stroke," she prodded.

The town busybodies again.

"He needed my encouragement to push through his exercises." Partly true.

"You gave up your dreams to care for your

dad. Be proud of that." Her big smile made him feel better, for a minute. "So what's wrong?"

"Two months ago I was offered a chance to return to college and get the degree I want," he blurted then nodded at her shocked expression. "Crazy bit is that a buddy of mine, we were going to college together, is now on the veterinarian faculty. He nominated me for a full scholarship in their new mature studies program. Starts in January."

"Full scholarship for vet school? That's fantastic." Elizabeth reached out and hugged him. A second later she pulled away, cheeks pink. "Sorry, but I'm thrilled for you. What does your dad say?"

"I haven't told him." Brett liked that hug. Too much. "I know I should have. I keep praying for the right way to say I want to leave his beloved ranch, knowing he can't manage the place on his own."

"Achieving your dream means crushing his." Elizabeth's immediate understanding touched him. "I'm so sorry, Brett. This should be the best news—"

"The best yet the worst," he agreed. "I want to have my dream, but I owe Dad everything, especially since I'm only now learning just how much he gave up to keep me when my mother left."

Elizabeth silently slid her hand in his and leaned toward him as if she couldn't wait to hear whatever he wanted to say. He admired Doc's giving spirit so much.

"Have you noticed how Dad opens up to Zoey?" Brett smiled when she rolled her eyes. "I overheard a part of their conversation last night, which made me ask questions around town. Dad always had an amazing voice. Still does."

"He should be the one leading the choir," Doc muttered then shrugged. "Go on."

"Turns out my father once auditioned for and won a coveted spot to go on tour with a well-known national choral group performing the *Messiah*. He found a renter for the ranch, sold some of his best cattle, was even buying a travel trailer so Mom and I could go with him when she announced she was leaving and taking me."

"Oh, no." She winced.

"This morning I learned that my Dad took every cent he'd raised, cleaned out his savings and gave it all to my mother. He gave up his dream of singing with that famous group so he could keep me."

"Your father loves you. Parents sacrifice for their kids, Brett." Elizabeth brushed his cheek with her fingers. "And you sacrificed your dream to go to college when Clint needed you. But that doesn't mean you should sacrifice again. Your dad would agree."

"I know. Even if it killed him, he'd insist I go." Brett turned his hand so her fingers were meshed with his, relishing the touch of her soft palm against his. "I don't know if I can do that, Doc."

"Because?"

"I don't have a bad life here. The ranch is doing fine. I've added my own interests. I've made it work," he said quietly, staring at her smooth oval nails. "I'm managing."

"That's what you want from life? To manage?" Her firm words demanded a reply.

"To make him happy—I owe him that."

"You owe your dad honesty," she said firmly. "I can't believe he'd want you to give up this opportunity and settle for a life of *managing*."

Brett said nothing. Elizabeth withdrew her hand from his, straightening as if she was girding herself for something unpleasant.

"May I tell you something personal?"

"Sure." Knowing more about Doc was exactly what Brett wanted.

"I was married for five years." Elizabeth couldn't look at him.

"To James." Brett nodded.

"Yes. We met in medical school. I planned to be an obstetrician. He wanted to be a plastic surgeon. I loved him very much but it was not a good marriage." Wasn't that an understatement? "I gave up my dream of women's medicine and worked as a general practitioner to put him through surgical residency. I didn't have the children I longed for because James said he wasn't ready. I worked long, draining hours at a hospital emergency room so James could take more and more specialty courses."

"Not very fair." Scorn laced Brett's voice.

"Fairness isn't part of James's world." Pain-filled memories cascaded through her mind. "At first I justified his constant criticism of me as constructive. Maybe I wasn't smart enough to study obstetrics, or be a full partner in the practice we started, though I worked far more hours than he did. Then his deprecation extended to everything I did. I learned to bury my dreams so I didn't have to listen to him castigate me for my failures. Eventually his belittling stopped me from doing most things I loved."

She slumped at what she'd given up for what she'd called "love."

"You don't need to say it." Brett's voice

tightened. "I can guess he's why you stopped singing in public."

"I directed a choir of handicapped kids. James hated it. Said I made a fool of myself with them, but I loved them. The day of their Christmas concert I got sick. I could barely walk but I couldn't disappoint them when they'd invited their entire families. So I directed, anyway." She gulped. "It was horrible. I couldn't hear properly to play and my pitch was way off for my solo." She saw only sympathy on Brett's face. "James was furious. He stole my joy in Christmas music. Those lovely notes always reminded me of James's scorn."

"You never directed since?"

"Not till now. I *managed.* Until now all I heard were his words of shame." She tried to smile. "I'm getting to the point."

"I'm listening, Doc."

Brett's caring nature—that was what would make him an amazing veterinarian. That was why she'd urge him not to give up his dream.

"When I became pregnant I was so happy. But James grew increasingly distant. The day Zoey arrived James sent our lawyer to the hospital to say he wanted a divorce. He had a mistress and she'd borne him a son. He wanted nothing to do with Zoey or me. Ever."

"Neither of you deserves a jerk like him." Brett's clenched jaw made her heart swell.

"Thank you." Elizabeth pressed on. "Anyway, while I was in the hospital James closed my part of the practice. My patients were directed elsewhere. Our joint accounts were emptied. I'd stupidly let him handle everything." She bit her lip. "The only thing he couldn't touch was my home because my parents had entailed it to me along with some money before we were married. They'd never approved of James. He showed up to rage about that the day I came home with Zoey."

"That's when he hit Rex." Brett squeezed her hand.

"Yes." She stifled a half sob. "Rex's death woke me up. I refused to sign the divorce agreement and hired a lawyer, an old friend from college who'd warned me years earlier about marrying James. She ensured my husband didn't leave me high and dry when all I could manage was tending my daughter and mourning Rex."

"God was caring for you," he said with a smile.

"I had to start over. I sold the house, left New York and when I was ready, worked part-time. On the fourth anniversary of Rex's death I cut my hair. My final act of defiance." She touched the very short strands. "Silly, isn't it?"

"Depends. James insisted on long hair?"

"He said it was the only thing that made me look halfway pretty." Why did that still hurt?

"I don't ever want to meet this stupid man." Brett's curling fist built a warm, tender feeling inside Elizabeth. How wonderful to have a defender.

"Thank you but he isn't worth it." She slid

her hand atop his fist and gave him a heart-felt smile.

"True." But anger still burned in Brett's narrowed gaze. Anger for her? Her heart turned to mush. What a sweet, caring man.

"James thought he'd won when I settled for less money. But it wasn't about money. It was about Zoey. Not knowing her, not seeing her grow and change, not feeling her hugs—he gave up all of that. I won the best part."

"Except the jerk left you a legacy of feeling like you're a failure," Brett spluttered then looked embarrassed.

"I'll survive." Elizabeth reminded herself she'd done nothing to be ashamed of, then stared directly into his eyes. "I never told Zoey about her father until recently because I didn't want her to grow up feeling like she's not enough. But I had to explain why she couldn't see him." She inhaled. "There was a point to pouring out my ugly personal details."

Brett let go of her hand as if to gather himself in preparation.

"You can't live your life *managing*, Brett. That's what I did for five years. I managed when I should have acted. Sooner or later *managing* takes its toll. Sometimes it's too late." She leaned forward to touch his jutting chin. "Talk to your dad," she pleaded. "Discuss it. Together you can find a way to work it out."

Brett slowly shook his head. "I can't."

Elizabeth slumped. She desperately wanted Brett to finally fulfill his dream.

And yet, deep inside, she wanted to beg him to stay in Snowflake, to be here to share things with her, to laugh with Zoey, to comfort and support and—wait a minute! She'd vowed never to risk her heart again. *Caution*, her brain screamed.

"The ranch is Dad's dream, Doc," Brett explained softly. "Everything he hoped for, planned and gave up his own dreams for. He'll be crushed if I leave." He smiled but angst darkened his mesmerizing eyes. "I want to go, but I have to think it through, pray, be certain that having my dream is worth hurting him so deeply."

Such compassion for the man who'd raised him moved her.

"You'll do the right thing," she murmured. "But you have to tell Clint soon. It would hurt him terribly if he found out from someone else that you're thinking of leaving."

"I know. I have to decide by December thirty-first." How could he choose between his father or his future?

Elizabeth knew Brett as a giver. But now she wanted this kind, gentle man to finally have his own heart's desire.

Yet inside her heart pleaded, *Please, don't go, Brett! Not now when our friendship has just begun.*

Friendship? Was that all they shared?

Chapter Six

For Brett, the afternoon's sleigh ride search for Christmas trees seemed part of a wistful daydream. Only it wouldn't end the way he imagined.

"The song says, 'In the meadow we can build a snowman,'" Zoey chanted. She glanced around. "Is this a meadow, CC?"

"Yep. Carlisle Meadow," Clint confirmed. "Stop the horses, son. It's snowman time. Zoey and I will build the bottom. C'mon, kid." He climbed out then lifted the little girl down while Brett slid his hands around Elizabeth's narrow waist and did the same. "You two get busy making the snowman's middle."

"Yes, sir!" Brett saluted then whispered, "Dad's acting like a kid."

"It's good for him, and you." Elizabeth's eyes sparkled as she scooped a handful of snow into her gloved hand. "Snowball fight?"

"Snow*man*," he emphasized, dodging the missile. When she scooped up more snow he glowered at her menacingly. "Don't think I won't wash your face just because you're a girl, Doc."

"As if you'd get the chance!" But she apparently rethought her intentions and began rolling a snowball on the ground. "How big do you want the middle, Zoey?"

"Huge!" Zoey's forehead furrowed as she glared at Clint. "You're s'posed to help."

"Yes, ma'am." He cleared a little spot with his shuffling feet then helped her begin the snowman's base. "Almost ready for his stomach, Brett. Get busy, boy."

"Bossy," Brett mumbled as he helped Elizabeth roll the second section over. Together they heaved it into place.

"Heavy." Doc's puffed breath formed a

white cloud around their heads. The sun reflected from her gold-striped ski suit enhancing the molten glints in her eyes. "Who's making the head?"

"All of us." Zoey tugged at Clint. "We'll start rolling and when it's big enough Mommy and Brett can put it on top."

"Good idea." His dad's smooth tenor voice joined hers in a song about reindeer.

Brett chuckled when Zoey chided Clint for mixing up the words.

"She's quite a girl, Doc," Brett said with a teasing wink. "Obviously your daughter."

"I'm not sure if that was meant as a compliment, but in the spirit of Christmas, I'll take it as one. I wish your dad was in our choir." She brushed his arm, directing his attention to Clint laughing at Zoey. Instead Brett's gaze locked with hers and suddenly everything around him faded.

This gorgeous woman was beautiful inside and out. He couldn't help wishing, hoping— for what? A relationship? But he planned to leave. What if he stayed and it didn't work out? What if he couldn't be what she wanted and she changed her mind, like Wanda had?

"What are you staring at?" Doc whispered.

"Your red nose." Without questioning his intent, Brett pressed a kiss against it. "Are you frozen?"

"Not anymore." Doc took a tiny step back, eyes flaring wide.

"Are you kissin' Mommy?" Zoey tugged on his pant leg, her eyes searching the boughs above them. "Is it 'cause that stuff over your heads is missing-toe?"

"Mistletoe, sweetie." Elizabeth dipped her head. When she dropped her hand from Brett's arm it felt like a physical loss—odd since he barely knew her.

Liar. You know Doc. You've never connected with any woman as you have with Elizabeth Kendall.

"Is it time to put on the snowman's head, Zoey?" He ignored the sudden burst of inner awareness.

"Yeah. Me 'n CC been waitin' for that." Zoey continued to study Brett. "You look funny."

"I've always told him that." Clint winked at Zoey but to Brett's dismay she stayed with her train of thought.

"Does kissin' make you feel funny?" she demanded.

"Ever got an Eskimo kiss?" Doc's startled look made Brett's face heat. But he had to do something to change the subject.

"No. How?" Zoey asked after a slight hesitation.

"Like this." He brushed her nose with his nose. "Does that kiss make you feel funny, Zoey?"

"Kinda." She repeated the gesture with Clint then shrugged. "What will we use for eyes and a nose on our snowman, CC?"

Brett's sigh of relief caught in his throat at Elizabeth's knowing grin.

"It's all your fault," he muttered, exasperated by the unruly feelings welling inside him.

"My fault that you kissed my nose?" She smacked her hands on her hips. "How?"

"You're too pretty." He stepped forward

and kissed her again, only this time it wasn't on the nose.

"Look, Zoey. They must have found some more missing-toe." Clint's barely suppressed mirth sobered Brett like a snow-wash to the face.

"Let's get this snowman finished." He employed the utmost restraint in not hauling Elizabeth into his arms for a repeat kiss despite their audience. "What're you using for eyes, kiddo?"

"Acorns," Zoey announced. "But we need arms."

Brett snapped off two twigs and inserted them. "Okay?"

"I guess. Buttons?" Her green eyes widened when he shook his head, as if surprised that he didn't carry snowman buttons in his pockets.

"The red berries on that bush might do." Elizabeth pointed, avoiding his gaze.

"Perfect." Brett retrieved several, which he planted down the front of the snowman.

"The birds will probably eat 'em," Clint said, head tilted to one side.

"You have another idea?" Brett felt desperate to escape Doc and the rush of confusing feelings whirling inside him. Since Clint didn't respond and Doc simply continued to study him with that enigmatic look she often wore to hide what she was really thinking, he suggested, "Into the sleigh and let's get back to Christmas tree hunting. Zoey, you sing 'Jingle Bells.'"

As they rode through the crisp afternoon, their voices echoing between the tall evergreens, Brett tried to ignore his overawareness of the woman seated next to him, but Doc's scent, soft and citrusy, brought back her words of this morning. He marveled anew that she'd taken on Snowflake's choir at all.

She'd endured so much and yet she still managed to give; to her daughter, her patients, the kids' choir, his dad. Elizabeth Kendall didn't wince from life. She took what she was given and made it into something wonderful. The evidence was Zoey, a daughter any parent would be proud of.

And yet, after this morning, Brett noticed a new reticence in Doc's manner toward him that made him wonder if she was fighting the same current of attraction that had snagged him in a whirlpool of contradictory feelings.

Refusing to let anything dampen their sleigh ride, Brett snapped the reins of his dad's favorite Appaloosas. With Zoey belting out her songs, Clint's horses, silver garlands around their necks, trotted smartly across the meadow toward the best spruce trees on the Double C.

Last week Pastor Bill had said God expected His children to have faith in Him to give the answers they needed. Brett had barely two weeks till Christmas. He hoped God would expedite His answer to the twin problems of college and what to do about his growing feelings for lovely Elizabeth Kendall.

Wearied by the fresh air and Zoey's persistent search for the perfect Christmas tree, Elizabeth gave thanks to finally be seated in front of the Carlisle fireplace. She hugged her knees, content to watch Zoey and Brett make tea.

"You look sleepy," Clint said.

"You have a fantastic voice. Why do you never sing in church, Clint?" Maybe she shouldn't have asked. She didn't want anything to ruin this special afternoon.

"Supposed to make a joyful noise to the Lord. Not a squawk," he joked.

"You need practice. Why don't you and Doc sing a duet?" Brett handed her a minty-scented mug. "Dad had the piano tuned last week."

The first time Elizabeth had entered the ranch house she'd glimpsed the old-fashioned upright sitting in the corner. On each return visit to the ranch her fingers had itched to play its ivory keys, knowing this piano maker had a quality of sound unrivaled by most upright pianos.

"I haven't played carols in years," she said hesitantly.

"You played Handel. You can play carols." Brett's faith in her lent confidence.

"Okay, but everyone sings." Maybe they would drown out her mistakes.

Clint barked, "I never said—"

Unable to deny herself Elizabeth sat and played a series of chords to get a feel for the instrument. The sound was glorious in the high-ceilinged room. "It's perfectly in tune."

"I'm guessing you have true pitch, like Dad?" Brett made a face when she nodded. "Is there anything you don't do well, Doc?"

She met his gaze, floundering in the wave of tenderness she felt for this kind man.

"I'm not good with animals. You've got the corner on that skill, Brett."

He didn't say anything, but he didn't break their stare, either. Not until Zoey demanded, "Are we gonna sing or what?"

Elizabeth tore her gaze from Brett's and launched into playing her daughter's favorite Christmas hymn, "Angels We Have Heard On High." Turned out Clint's tenor was a perfect foil for Brett's baritone on the "Glorias."

"Sing your part, Mommy," Zoey insisted, Mrs. Beasley cuddled in her arms.

And since her heart felt light and care-free, Elizabeth gave her voice free rein as she reached for the high soprano harmony notes, something she hadn't done in a very long time. Despite her awareness of Brett at her elbow, she reveled in the lovely words of the old carols telling of God's gift to the world. Her delight for the Christmas music she'd always adored returned as she played carol after carol, allowing the glorious music to soothe her heart until it felt right to let the last notes die away.

"Thank you, Elizabeth. I enjoyed that." Clint sounded introspective as he returned to his seat on the sofa.

"So did I." Brett touched her shoulder in a too-fleeting caress. "Thank you for giving us such a wonderful Christmas memory."

Elizabeth knew he was thinking of the opportunity he'd been offered and that he and his father might not share another Christmas on the Double C. She rose, surprised to see a tear on his lashes. Unthinking she reached out and lifted it with her fingertip.

"I haven't heard him sing like that in years," he said for her ears alone. "It's the very best Christmas gift anyone could have given me, Doc." As she stared into his eyes she thought she could almost hear his inner argument.

How can I leave him? But how can I give up my dream?

She desperately wanted to comfort Brett, to ease the torture of having to make such a difficult choice. But the debacle of her marriage made her wary of getting involved. She'd fought hard to rebuild her world, to build a new life, to be all that Zoey needed. Today she'd caught a glimpse of the inner woman she'd once been, wanted to be again.

How could she risk it all by letting herself care for another man, even one as special as Brett Carlisle? Yet the more she shared special moments like today with him, the more she longed to give in to the yearning to slip into his arms.

"When can Mrs. Beasley come home with us, Mommy?" Zoey asked.

Ah, the puppy. Proof positive that Elizabeth hadn't made as much progress as she thought when she was still haunted by the image of poor Rex in her arms, drawing in his last pained breaths. It was a reminder of everything she would be wise not to forget—that love could quickly turn to something else.

"Honey, I don't—"

"Zoey, let's make pizza." Once again it was Brett to the rescue, engaging her daughter in making dinner. He was such a great guy, a sensitive, gentle man you could count on.

Except she couldn't count on Brett because he was leaving Snowflake. In her heart Elizabeth knew he wouldn't be able to refuse his dream and that she didn't have the strength to survive losing at love again.

Shaking free of the gloomy thoughts, Elizabeth conferred with Clint about the Christmas Eve program.

"All great ideas. But can you think of anything we could use as instruments? Like bells or…something?" she asked hopefully.

"I think the kids can manage five songs, but even with congregational singing and your readings, it's not enough."

"I had an idea about that." Brett left Zoey peering into the oven, watching the pizza cook as she cradled the sleeping puppy. "Remember when you got to play those metal triangles as a kid? They kind of sound like bells."

"But we don't have any of those. Do we?" His expression intrigued Elizabeth.

"I could make them." Brett described his father's small forge. "Then every kid could play along, keeping the beat as you played the song."

"That would be amazing." *You're helping me, God,* her heart whispered. Yet she was still afraid to let hope take over. What if she failed again? "We need at least thirty triangles and we don't have much time until Christmas Eve," she reminded.

"I made a test sample. Want to hear?" At her wide-eyed nod, he walked to the door, opened a cabinet beside it and removed a shiny metal triangle. "Zoey, come and play this for us."

Green eyes huge, Zoey eased Mrs. Beasley onto the floor then walked over. "How do I play it?"

"Sing a song and tap it as you sing." Elizabeth snuck a glance at Brett as Zoey launched into "Silent Night," her little baton keeping time to the music, filling the room with a happy tinkling.

"Was that okay?" Zoey asked.

"Okay?" Brett snatched her into his arms, whirled her around then kissed her cheek. "It was stupendous, fantastic, amazing." He glanced at Elizabeth. "Wasn't it?"

"Stupendous, fantastic, amazing," she repeated. Maybe, thanks to Brett, she wasn't going to totally ruin Snowflake's Christmas Eve kids' choir. "We just need another twenty-nine."

"Is the pizza ready?" Zoey squealed, wiggling free. "Can we eat?"

They sat at the table, heads bowed, while Clint said Grace. A stray thought fluttered.

What would it be like to be able to count on Brett all the time? To share every day with him?

What would life be like when he left Snowflake?

Oh, Lord, guard my heart.

Chapter Seven

"You look tired, Doc." A week later Brett hid his shock.

Elizabeth bore dark circles under her eyes. The erect line of her shoulders seemed to bow with weariness. His arms ached to hold her until she regained the persistent courage he'd come to expect in her sparkling gaze.

But he had no right.

"I've had a few sleepless nights. Why do kids still drink and drive?" She failed to smother a yawn.

"The Mueller boy." He nodded. "I heard it was touch and go and that you saved his life."

"I did my job. God did the rest." She

glanced around the sanctuary. "It's Saturday morning. Why aren't the kids here for practice?"

"About that—I left you a message yesterday. You didn't get it? I don't suppose anyone thought to tell you that today is Snowflake's annual ice sculpture contest. The kids are competing for some nice prizes."

"But what about practice?" The fear in Doc's hazel eyes touched a nerve deep inside him. She was scared. "Without practice this thing will be a flop."

"No, it won't." *Right, Lord?* "It is going to be a huge success." Brett brushed his knuckles across her cheek. "Go home and take a nap. I rescheduled practice for seven, after the ice sculpture judging."

"I can't nap. Mrs. House has this afternoon off. I have to get Zoey." She rubbed her neck as if stiffness had set in.

Without thinking Brett stepped behind her and set his fingers against her shoulder blades, gently working out the tension.

"I'll take care of Zoey. You go home and

rest." His senses sang, which meant he had to stop touching her. He pressed her shoulders to force her to turn then lifted her chin to meet his gaze. "For once relax and let me handle it."

"Once? I've been doing that so much I don't know how you get any work done at your ranch." Her gaze clung to his.

"Dad will chew me out if I slack off too much." Brett didn't mention he'd risen to do chores at four this morning so he'd be free if she needed him. "I won't let you down, Elizabeth," he assured her, his pulse thudding like a base drum.

"You never do, Brett. But what if I mess up again?"

"That's James speaking," he said, drawing her into his arms for a brief hug. "And he's wrong. We've got God on our side and the choir's going to be amazing." He let her go, waited for her to regain her poise and heaved a sigh of relief when a tremulous smile flickered across her lovely face.

"I don't know what I'd do without you,"

she whispered. "You're God's blessing in my life, Brett."

Catching him totally unawares, Doc stood on her tiptoes and kissed him right on the lips. It wasn't a deep, soulful kiss nor a mere brush of the lips. It said—no, asked—something Brett couldn't quite define. And when it ended, he wanted more.

"I accept your offer with Zoey. Thank you." Then without looking at him, Doc buttoned up her coat, slipped on her gloves and left the sanctuary.

Brett stifled the urge to call her back. *He was in love with her!*

The truth echoed from his heart. He loved Doc's spirit, her faith in him, her gentleness and her courage. He loved the way she forged ahead despite the nasty hand she'd been dealt. But Brett *couldn't* love her—because he'd finally decided to leave Snowflake, to grab his opportunity.

He couldn't start his college degree and expect Elizabeth to wait years until he finished. Nor could he expect her to uproot herself and her daughter just when she'd begun rebuilding her life. It wasn't fair to ask her to toss it all away for his dream, not like James had. Brett would never ask Elizabeth to sacrifice what she'd worked so hard to achieve. Besides, what if he failed? What if the classes were too difficult for him, the instructors too demanding? Beyond all that, a long-distance relationship, stretched over years of him in school—no.

Brett couldn't love her.

Except he already did. He loved Elizabeth Kendall. No matter what he did, that wasn't going to change. So loving her meant he had one option, which was to do as much as he could to help her with the kids' choir, to help her shed the lack of confidence she battled. After Christmas he'd leave, but if he could help Doc succeed with the choir, maybe its success would help her become an integral part of Snowflake so she'd feel needed, wanted, able to give.

So she'll be here if you come back?

Brett had to acknowledge that had been in

the back of his mind. It was foolish but he couldn't quite let go of the dream of Doc and Zoey in his world.

A noise behind him made him turn.

"Brett, I'm glad you're still here. You've been on my mind a lot this past week. Is there something you're struggling with?" Pastor Bill frowned at him. "Anything I can do to help?"

"No, thanks. I—" Brett changed his mind. "Actually I could use your prayers. I'm considering some big changes in my life and I could use God's guidance."

"Clint didn't mention—"

"He doesn't know. No one does." Brett waited, hoping he'd understand.

"Then I'll keep it between us and the Lord as I pray for you, son." The senior man frowned. "I feel led to repeat a verse that's been rolling through my mind this week. I'm sure you know it well. 'Trust in the Lord with all your heart and lean not to your own understanding. In all your ways acknowledge Him and He will direct your paths.'"

"I do know it. And I needed to be reminded. Thanks, Pastor." Brett smiled his appreciation. "I guess I'd better go. I promised Doc I'd watch Zoey this afternoon."

He discovered Mrs. House had taken Zoey to the school yard so she could compete in the ice sculpture contest. While watching, Brett was surprised to hear some of the kids grouse that they were tired of working so hard at choir practice.

He pulled out his phone. Maybe he and Clint could help Doc by adding a little fun to the practice tonight.

Elizabeth hadn't expected to feel so rested after just a few hours' sleep and it wasn't only because she knew Brett would take good care of Zoey. Perhaps her relaxation had to do with her dreams of him; crazy, happy scenarios of building snowmen, skating on the ice rink that now filled the town square and kissing under a Christmas star.

She certainly didn't expect to find the handsome cowboy and his dad with the choir kids, in front of the church, building a manger scene in the snow.

"You've been busy," she said, unable to smother her burst of joy.

"Isn't it nice, Mommy?" Zoey was breathless. "Brett said we hafta decorate the front of the church. An' then we're gonna put up a big sign about our concert for ad-tizing. Isn't Brett smart? An' CC's gonna put lights so everybody can see Baby Jesus and his mom and dad when it's dark. It's gonna be stupendulous."

"Stupendous," Elizabeth corrected gently. "It sure is. Who made the camels?"

"Brett an' Ernie. Brett knows all kinds 'a stuff 'bout camels like 'zackly where to put the hump an' what kinda toes to make." Zoey dragged her by the hand to inspect every element, but Elizabeth caught herself inspecting Brett most of all.

"It's lovely." She congratulated Clint on his work. "I guess you'll light the Christmas tree, too?"

"I'll put the lights on it but we don't turn

them on until Christmas Eve, after the concert." The old man winked. "It's tra—"

"—dition," she finished with a laugh, her
heart racing when Brett's chuckle joined
hers. "There certainly are a lot of them in
Snowflake."

"Traditions are what make families and
communities." Clint glanced at Brett. A tiny
frown creased his forehead. "It's what binds
us together."

Her heart winced at the look that washed
over Brett's face. How difficult the next ten
days would be for him. And for Clint.

Please tell him. Elizabeth hoped he heard
her mental plea. Clint would need time to
work out his own future, one without his son
and perhaps the ranch he loved.

"Pizza's here," Brett called as a car drove
up. "Let's finish up and go have supper. Then
you'll really be able to sing."

It was an inspired idea. A surge of joy almost swamped Elizabeth as she listened to
her choir chat about the need to sing their
very best. *Her choir?*

"It's Your choir, Lord," she murmured.

"We made the outside of the church look good," one boy said. "We better make sure we sound just as good."

"You will," Brett encouraged with a grin. His smile made her toes curl. "Doc's got a surprise for you tonight so hurry."

The entire group, even Zoey, studied her curiously as they added the final details before trooping inside. Elizabeth hung back.

"Um, what's my surprise, Brett?" she murmured curiously.

"The triangles are ready to debut and so are the kids' costumes." He chuckled at her stare. "I think you'll like both."

Elizabeth managed to swallow a few bites of Hawaiian pizza while silently praying that Mabel hadn't made good on her threat to sew frilly gold tinsel angel costumes and that the kids could master using Brett's triangles. Her fear of failing to pull off the kids' concert and especially her own solo dragged at her spirit like lead. Why couldn't she trust God? Why did she still hear James's mocking voice in the back of her head, reminding her of that last Christmas concert?

You thought you could do it and you failed. You ruined everything.

"Ready?" Brett's touch on her arm jerked her out of the shame. Forcing a smile, she rose. "I'd say Dad's ice-cream cake was a success, wouldn't you?" He smiled at the red-and-green-tinged mouths around the table.

"So much better than fruitcake," she agreed then grinned. "And I don't care if fruitcake is a tradition in Snowflake. So there."

"It isn't," Brett shouted with laughter. "Oh, Doc, you've changed from the meek and mild lady who first took on this choir."

"I wish," she shot back. "Inside I'm shaking."

"Maybe Pastor was thinking of you, too." Brett gathered debris from the table.

"Huh?" She frowned at him.

"He reminded me of a verse today. 'Trust in the Lord with all your heart and lean not to your own understanding. In all your ways acknowledge Him and He will direct your paths.' See what I mean?"

A current ran through those dark eyes of his, holding her breath prisoner.

"You and I both need to stop fussing about stuff and trust God to work it out," he added.

"Easier said than done." Elizabeth had to ask, "Have you told your dad yet?"

He shook his head without looking at her. "I need the right moment."

"Brett—" She let him walk away without reminding him that time was short. Telling Clint was his business. She knew he'd do the best for his father, yet she clung to the hope that he'd change his mind about leaving Snowflake.

How silly was that?

"Mommy, me and Ariana wanna know what the s'prise is." Zoey's auburn head tilted to one side. "Is it 'bout you an' Brett?"

"What? No." Elizabeth studied her daughter's disappointed face. "Why would you think that?"

"'Cause you an' Brett look at each other

funny." Head dropping, voice brimming with disappointment, she murmured, "I thought maybe God was gonna give me a daddy for Christmas." A tear trickled down her cheek. "Isn't He gonna give me anything I want?"

Elizabeth hugged her daughter close, assuring her that God would give her His very best. It seemed Brett wasn't the only one who needed to have a family talk.

"You and I will discuss this later, okay?" She smoothed away the tears from Zoey's cheek. "Remember that I love you, sweetie. Now, let's go practice."

"'Kay." Sniffing, Zoey took her place in the front row of the choir.

"Okay, guys. Here's one of the surprises." Brett nodded to Mabel, who held up a red velvet cape with a big white satin bow. "This is what you'll be wearing on Christmas Eve when you sing your songs."

"They're so pretty," one of the senior girls said. "We'll match but we won't look silly."

"My mom has a picture of old-fashioned carolers. That looks like what they wore.

Cool." A younger boy grinned. "We gotta sing really good now."

"They're lovely, Mabel. Absolutely perfect. Thank you." Elizabeth hugged Mabel, who couldn't stop grinning as she left. "Children, let's make our music sound as good as we'll look. Brett's made us something to help."

She watched him pass out the shiny triangles strung with green ribbon. Then he showed the kids how to tap the baton against the metal to get the sound. The next half hour was spent trying to perfect a beat. And failing. Elizabeth was about to give up when Zoey's friend Ariana let out a piercing whistle that silenced the entire group.

"Listen," she said, her cheeks red with irritation. "This is s'posed to sound like bells. *Ding, ding, ding.* Like in that movie, *Home Alone*, when the kid runs home to stop the bad guys. You know, *Hark how the bells, sweet silver bells*—now pay 'tention."

Startled gazes moved from the little girl to Elizabeth, who forced down her amusement at Ariana's battle tone, delighted with the idea she'd just provided.

"Ariana's right. Touch the triangle once so we hear one sharp *ting* on the beat. But watch me so you'll know when. When my hand moves like this, you ting. Okay?" Most of the group nodded. "Let's try it."

Moments later they had it, a semi-cohesive sound that made Elizabeth smile with delight. She turned to share her joy with Brett, who stood watching her from the back of the church. To her surprise his face looked sober, even sad.

"Help us, Brett." She beckoned him forward. "I'm going to play. You count out the rhythm and motion down for them to play on the first and fourth beat."

"Listen, Doc, I don't do—"

"Wasn't it you who was just telling me to trust God to work it out?" she reminded.

When he finally nodded, Elizabeth hid her relief as she walked to the piano.

"Everybody ready?" They lifted their instruments. "I'll start. Watch Brett. He'll show you when you should play. Here we go." She launched into an introduction of "Carol of the Bells." "Go," she called and waited for the chimes.

It took several starts, which clearly revealed Brett's frustration. Finally Clint yelled, "Stop!" He walked over to Brett and murmured something to him. His hand moved in a beat that measured the tempo she'd been playing. Brett copied it.

"Ready to start again?" she called when Clint had returned to his pew.

"I guess," Brett muttered. Elizabeth caught Clint's wink before he lifted his hand as if he, too, would follow the beat.

So Brett could copy, she suddenly realized as this time the chimes hit every beat.

"Perfect! You guys are fantastic!" She nodded her thanks at Brett then set out her sheet music. "If you do that well on your singing, we'll have a fantastic performance."

It turned into one of the best rehearsals they'd ever had.

"Thanks to both of you," Elizabeth told father and son as the children were picked up by their parents. "Your instruments made the difference, Brett." She hugged Clint. "And your help got them all playing together. For the first time I'm beginning to think we might pull this off."

"So your faith is overcoming your fear?" Brett asked softly.

"I guess." But for how long, Elizabeth wondered later that night when she wakened from nightmares of that other Christmas concert and the humiliation she'd endured.

This is Your will, isn't it? she whispered.

The choir, maybe. But Brett in her life? Elizabeth felt no certainty about that.

Chapter Eight

One week until Christmas. This had to be the day.

Brett gathered his courage and cleared his throat, glad Clint had made his uber-strong coffee for breakfast this morning. Maybe that would give him the courage he needed.

"Dad, can I talk to you about something?"

"Been wondering when you'd get around to it." Clint stretched out his legs and studied his boot tips. "It's about the college scholarship, isn't it?"

"You know?" Brett blinked in surprise. "Since when?"

"Since that first day when your friend

called." Despite his shrug of nonchalance his dad's tension was evident. "I was in the barn and heard the phone so I picked up the extension and heard your friend offer you a scholarship. Didn't mean to butt into your business."

"Why didn't you say anything?" Brett asked, thoughts jumbled.

"Figured you'd get around to telling me when you were ready." Clint did look at him then. "Veterinarian school is what you always wanted so I guess you're going."

"I don't know." No fight? No argument? Brett lost his breath like a pricked balloon. "It's a dream I never thought I'd realize."

"Here's your chance. Go." Clint's *careless* attitude made Brett wonder why he'd worried so much about his father's reaction.

"If I accepted, what would you do—about the ranch, I mean?"

"I've got options." Clint shifted so Brett couldn't see his face. One hand rubbed a spot on the back of his neck. Noting Brett's attention it quickly dropped away. "Jeremiah

Bremmer's been asking to buy my Black Angus herd. He'd rent the back forty, too. Or maybe I'll sell the place, move into town."

"You? In town?" Brett couldn't envision it.

"Can't stay here forever." Clint shrugged. "Be a test of faith. God's always come through for me before."

Meaning his son's leaving didn't matter.

"I'd come back to help when school's out," he said quickly then added, "If you want."

"No point in tying yourself down to the Double C or Snowflake." Clint looked totally unconcerned. "Besides, we got Doc Terrier. Town doesn't need another vet."

Brett had considered entering a partnership with Snowflake's vet when he finished college. His dad's comment made him wonder how many of the locals would accept him as qualified. They'd always known him as Clint's kid, a rancher like them, not an educated veterinarian.

"Better you start over someplace fresh," the old man suggested. "I'm too old for that. My friends, what's left of 'em, are here." A coy smile played with his mouth. "'Sides, I'm kinda taken with that little Zoey. Never knew a kid so full of sass and spice. Reminds me of myself. I'd like to watch her grow up, sorta like a grandfather. She hasn't got one, you know."

"Ah." His dad wanted to be a *grandfather*?

"Doc and Zoey don't have any other family." Evidently the two ladies had found a soft spot in Clint's crusty heart. "Anyway, let me know your decision so I can plan."

That's it? Brett wanted to yell.

"Guess I'll go check on that mare." Clint loaded his dishes in the dishwasher. "Jessie Endstrom wants the colt. Offered me a good price. I'll probably sell him all the horses."

"Even Sheba?" He couldn't believe this. "You've had her since she was born!"

"She's getting old and she needs to be ridden more often. Prob'ly for the best." His father dragged on his sheepskin jacket, his hand rubbing his neck again. "Decision's yours, son. Just let me know. I'm goin' to town later. I'll have lunch there."

Stunned, Brett watched his father leave. That hadn't gone as he expected. Far from asking, no, begging, him to stay, Clint had almost helped him out the door.

He cleared up the breakfast remains, restoring the nook to tidiness, reminded of the many times he and his father had shared things across this very table. Leaving the ranch wasn't going to be easy for him, but it was going to be much harder for his father, no matter how casual he acted.

Is this right? he prayed as he pulled on his warmest gear, preparing to check fences on the back range before they got more snow. *Am I making a big mistake? But then why would You send this opportunity? What's the best decision for us both, God?*

As Brett trotted his horse across the pasture and headed north Elizabeth's face swam into his thoughts. Not to see her again, not to be there if she and Zoey needed him… What if Doc began to doubt herself again? The choir's progress seemed to have rebuilt her confidence but what if Zoey's dad came back for some reason? Or what if Elizabeth met someone else?

Man, Brett hated that thought. She was his.

But she wasn't. He had no claim on Elizabeth. There was nothing to keep her from building a new friendship with someone who would be here for her and Zoey.

As he repaired fences, ate his sandwich and drank coffee from his thermos, scanned the hills for predators and checked cattle, two questions rolled through Brett's brain.

How could he leave his home and the woman who'd taken root in his heart?

But how could he give up the opportunity to have his dream come true?

He had no answers. All he could do was pray.

"Why doesn't he answer?" Elizabeth demanded of her cell phone.

"Who?" Zoey looked up from her plate of spaghetti, her face a mess of red sauce.

"Brett." She sighed, rose and scraped her uneaten meal into the garbage, trying to stem the tide of doubt that had taken root this morning after she'd treated six children with severe cases of the flu.

"Maybe he's sick. Three kids in my class had to go home today. Everybody's getting sick. Even Mrs. House. I hope Mrs. Beasley doesn't get sick," Zoey said with a frown. "Do dogs get the flu?"

"I don't know, sweetheart." *If I ever get hold of Brett you can ask him.* "You'd better go wash up. We have choir practice tonight." *If anybody shows.*

Why wouldn't these doubts leave her? She'd tried so hard to turn everything over to God, to do what she could and leave the outcome to Him. And yet, especially after what Elizabeth had learned today, she couldn't quite shake this dark cloud of worry.

If I truly trust God, worry has no place in my heart. Elizabeth whispered a plea for forgiveness as she cleaned up the kitchen.

"The choir is yours, God. The Christmas Eve service is Yours. You are in control. I will do my part to glorify You." Saying it aloud chased away some of the doubt, though bits of misgiving lingered on the fringes of her mind.

When they arrived at the church and found only half the usual number of children present, Elizabeth's misgivings returned tenfold, accompanied by the memory of past repudiation.

You think saying you're a Christian means God will fix anything you take on. Then you fail and wonder why. You don't have Superwoman abilities, Lizzie. You're not specially called out by God Himself. You're ordinary, nothing special. Plain. And you mess up more things than anyone I've ever known. You're embarrassing.

She surveyed the small group of kids and wondered if maybe James was right.

"Sorry I'm late. Had a problem with a steer." Brett stood in the doorway of the sanctuary, his smile fading. "Where is everybody?"

"They gots flu." Zoey grinned at him. "But we don't."

"Oh, boy." Brett walked slowly forward, his gaze holding Elizabeth's so she couldn't look away. "Dad's down with something, too. Came on late this afternoon, I guess. He seems really depressed." He didn't have the usual warmth in his eyes so she was surprised when he came close enough to touch her shoulder. "How are you feeling?"

"Me? I'm fine, but—maybe we should cancel this," she murmured, turning to shield her words from the kids who waited.

"No!" Brett's eyes narrowed. "You can't give up, Doc."

"Aren't we gonna sing, Mommy?" Zoey's plaintive question held the other kids' focus. "We've been practicing really hard. And we got those nice covers to wear an' the bells an' everything. We gotta sing!"

The rest of the choir nodded, faces resolute.

"How can you naysay faith like that?" Brett whispered in her ear.

"I can't." She heaved a sigh of resignation. "Okay, let's get at it. Brett, you'll have to take your father's part because we need to practice our entrances."

"That's why I'm here." His dazzling smile turned her knees to jelly before he walked to the side and arranged his readings. "I'm ready."

Nervous, uncertain yet somehow steadied by Brett's confidence in her, Elizabeth waited for the recorded music to start. *The choir is Yours. I'll do my best for You.* Then she lifted her hand to direct the small group.

The kids did their best, came in at the proper time, sang lustily and smiled constantly. They were doing everything right. Even the chiming of the triangles was on the beat. It was just that the sound they made seemed weak in the large sanctuary.

"This is where you sing your solo, isn't it?" Brett asked. "Why not rehearse it now?"

With everyone watching? Elizabeth gulped but nodded. If she was going to trust God, then she had to trust Him with everything. She leaned to one side, pressed a button to start the recorded music then exhaled.

She knew her first notes wobbled, heard the tentative sound in her voice and the feebleness as she stretched to reach the highest note. A tiny movement to her left caught her eye. Brett smiled at her, encouraging her to give her best.

Elizabeth tried to infuse her song with all the heartfelt feeling it deserved. But the entire time she sang she heard James's voice. *Embarrassing. Ashamed.* The words held her back, warning her she would be mocked. As she finished she glanced at Zoey, knowing her daughter wouldn't be able to hide the truth. Sure enough Zoey's little face was troubled.

"You have to practice harder, Mommy," she insisted. "We hafta do our very bestest to celebrate Jesus's birthday."

"You're right, sweetie." She smiled, struggling to infuse certainty in her voice when all she felt was a horrible cloying fear of failure. "Now Clint reads another part. Brett?"

He studied her with uncertainty, his dark gaze troubled, as if he, too, wondered if she could pull it off. Regrouping he read the appropriate section and the practice continued. Elizabeth caught herself hurrying the children, eager to get the rehearsal finished so she could get Zoey into bed and finally be alone. Maybe then she could figure out what was wrong.

"Okay, guys. That's all for now." She called a halt when they'd barely finished the last song. "One more practice then a dress rehearsal when we go through everything exactly as we will on Christmas Eve. Stay healthy so you can sing your best."

"An' 'vite lots of people," Zoey commanded. "We're gonna sing good."

"Yes, you are," Brett agreed with a smile. "And everyone will love it. Let's pray before you leave."

I should have thought of that, Elizabeth thought guiltily. She bowed her head, listening as Brett asked God to bless their efforts, to heal those who were sick and help them to remember Jesus was the reason for Christmas, the reason they were singing.

When he finished, Elizabeth busied herself with organizing her sheet music to avoid the accusation she knew she'd find in his eyes. Her head jerked up when he chuckled at something one of the kids said.

"No, it wasn't our best practice but that means we can do better, right?" His carefree laugh when they shouted back an exuberant "Yes!" made her frown.

"You look cranky," he said as Zoey gathered up the triangles. "What's wrong?"

"Didn't you hear me?" she asked, suddenly furious. "I sounded like a cat in pain. I'm going to be mortified when this thing is finished. And it's all your fault."

Brett studied her with that unflappable stare.

"Well?" she demanded.

"It's not about you, or me or them," he said quietly. "It's about Him." He pointed upward. "Remember?"

"He's going to be ashamed, too," she mumbled, ducking her head in humiliation.

"Doc," Brett gently chastised, pressing his

finger under her chin to force her to look at him. "You know that's not right. He takes our efforts and uses them for His will, to work out things His way."

How could he say that? Didn't he understand? She really looked at him then. Something had changed. Brett looked lighter, more carefree.

"I spoke to my dad this morning, Doc." His eyes glowed. "He knew about the scholarship and he's all in favor of me going. He's talking about selling the ranch and moving into town."

"He'll have to," she said automatically, her mind mentally scanning the report she'd seen.

"He even sounded happy about selling the stock and renting out his land to a neighbor. He—" Brett stopped suddenly, frowned. "Wait a minute—why'd you say that? Why would he have to?"

Catching the flu might be the reason Clint hadn't told him but Elizabeth guessed his father was deliberately hiding the truth from his son. And she couldn't say anything, not a word, or she'd breach patient confidentiality, if she hadn't already.

"So you've decided to leave for college, after all?" Funny how the thought of not seeing Brett, not being able to depend on him for support and courage—made her feel empty. Alone.

"Yes, but—"

"You must be very excited. Congratulations. I wish you much success." She focused on Zoey, struggling to put on her boots. "We'll miss you. Thank you for all your help. Excuse me."

She wanted to get away before she burst into tears. Instead she knelt and helped her daughter slide on her boots only to rise and find Brett holding her coat. When she shrugged into it, he turned her around and began fastening the buttons.

"I'm going to miss you, too, Doc. You give me a new perspective on life." He rested his palms on her shoulders. "Thanks to you I've figured out what I want."

"I'm glad." Elizabeth ached to fling her arms around Brett's neck and beg him not to leave Snowflake. But she couldn't ask him not to grab at his dream. And she couldn't tell him that his father had cancer. All she could do for this man she loved was silently care for him and be there for his dad.

"I wanted to tell you—"

"Can we go home, Mommy? My tummy feels funny."

"Another time." Brett brushed his lips against her cheek.

"Sure," Elizabeth agreed, willing herself not to turn her head and return his kiss. As she drove home she determined to smother her feelings for the handsome rancher and do everything she could to make this Christmas the best Brett and his father ever had.

Don't let it be their last, God. Please?

Chapter Nine

"Something's wrong with Dad." Brett faced his pastor the next morning and laid bare his aching heart. "Doc knows. I asked her to tell me but she won't."

"She can't."

"But I need to know. This is my father!" Brett winced at the thought of losing his only parent.

"I just have secondhand information about this, son. I'm going to share it because I believe you should know. Clint should be telling you, but since he hasn't—" Pastor Bill squeezed his eyes closed in a silent prayer before he looked directly at Brett.

"It's bad, isn't it?" He sucked in his breath when the pastor, his face grave, nodded. He exhaled. "Okay. Tell me."

"Your father has an aggressive form of skin cancer. He needs immediate surgery and treatment."

Brett gasped in stunned disbelief. "But—" He couldn't grasp it, couldn't make sense of it. Of all the things he'd imagined, cancer hadn't even made the list.

"He doesn't want you to know." The minister squeezed his shoulder. "Clint thinks he has to push through this alone. He intends to divest himself of the home, land and animals he loves to focus on his treatment." His voice dropped. "And free you from having to care for him."

"But why Dad? He's healthy except for the stroke—was that what did it?"

Questions poured out but Pastor Bill didn't have the answers Brett needed. The only thing Bill could offer was to listen and then to pray with him.

Two hours later Brett left the church office, still in a turmoil, still unable to absorb it. *Cancer.* He wandered around town facing the knowledge that his father might not be here next time he came home. That he might die. He tried to pray but his heart only cried, *Why?*

"Brett?" Elizabeth's voice and the touch of her fingers on his arm brought him back to reality. "Are you all right?"

"No," he said softly. "How can I be? Pastor Bill just told me my father is dying."

"He— You don't know that..." Elizabeth stopped when he shook his head. He didn't want to hear platitudes.

"You knew about his diagnosis," he said bluntly. "You knew and you didn't tell me."

"I happened to see his lab report, but I couldn't tell you, Brett. You know my professional oath doesn't allow that."

"I know." He felt as if his world had cracked. "But..."

"I have the afternoon off. Let's have lunch and talk." She slipped her hand through his arm.

With the sun gilding her silvery hair and her high-heeled boots skimming over the slippery sidewalks, Doc looked like something out of this world, certainly out of *Brett's* world. He accompanied her to the nearest café, sat where she indicated and let her order two soups and a sandwich to split. When it arrived, Brett ate because she insisted.

"Tell me your thoughts," she murmured when he'd finished the soup.

"That I must have really angered God." Fear, hurt and bitterness surged inside him. "I've tried hard to be the son Dad deserves but I've never done anything noteworthy and now I never will."

"You do realize you're quoting Wanda?" She arched a brow. "So I'll tell you the same thing you once told me about James—you've still got her somewhere in here." Doc tapped his forehead, her cheeks hot pink in annoyance. "You still believe her lies."

Brett loved the way she defended him, the way her hair curled around her cheeks in a caress, the way she didn't skip over the important stuff; in short, he loved everything about Dr. Elizabeth Kendall. But he wasn't rich or smart like her ex.

He blinked as his brain caught up to her words. "Lies?"

"They were lies, Brett. She was just like James."

He frowned at the comparison. "How?"

"When we met, James's driving goal was to become a surgeon to help scarred children. As a kid his best friend had burn scars no one could remove. James wanted to be able to do that."

Brett's heart sank. She was comparing him to a surgeon?

"I loved that," she murmured. "It's why I put off my own dreams and worked extra hours, so he could become that doctor."

He waited warily.

"But James got caught up in money and prestige. He began replacing free clinic time with paid-for nose jobs." The sadness in her voice mirrored the grief in her eyes. "James was drinking when he got a call. He was hurrying to an appointment with a twenty-eight-year-old celebrity who wanted a chin lift. Rex died because of James's greed."

There was nothing to say so Brett slid his hand over hers and held it.

"James became someone I didn't know. Zoey and I didn't mean anything to him." Elizabeth blinked. "Just like Wanda."

"Wanda?" He didn't get it.

"She was a teacher and a good one from what I've heard. She must have liked teaching kids once. But her focus got skewed. A guy who loved her wasn't enough. She changed. Like you have."

"I'm nothing like Wanda or your ex, Doc." Brett's shoulders went back indignantly.

"We all get sidetracked." She shook her head. "Like I did with Rex."

"*I* haven't changed." Doc's enigmatic expression intrigued Brett.

"Haven't you?" Her eyes said different. "When I first met you I thought, wow, here's a guy who makes his faith work. He encourages and builds up and makes people's lives better. He loves animals so he finds way to improve their worlds, too. His dad's a grump and they don't share the same dream, but Brett works the spread as if it were his own. The kids' choir needs a leader so he cons me into helping. Props needed? He builds them." She smiled. "I thought, Brett does what he can and trusts God with the rest. This guy has faith figured out."

"Reality sucks, huh?"

"Reality's even better." She smiled. "That's why I fell in love with you."

"What?" Brett stared.

"I never wanted to but you've shown me what real love is. You helped me understand that though I loved Rex dearly, I *can* open my heart to another dog." She touched his cheek tenderly. "We are taking Mrs. Beasley, by the way. Only don't tell Zoey yet."

"Elizabeth, I—" There were a thousand things Brett wanted to say, mostly that he loved her, too. But after her praise how could he admit he wanted to run far and fast? That he was scared to trust God in case He took Clint, scared to grab his dream and scared not to? How could he admit that the faith she admired was a sham?

"I had to tell you that so you'd know Wanda was wrong." She winked. "If we got do-overs in life she'd probably choose James. But I wouldn't. I'd choose you, Brett, because you don't talk about love, you *do* love."

Totally nonplussed by her honesty, he swallowed. This woman, this amazing woman.

"You don't have to say you love me, Brett. I know you do. You show it in everything you do. That's enough for me." Her hand turned, her fingers meshing with his as her hazel eyes held him immobile. "Right now you think God's abandoned you, stolen your dream. But He hasn't. 'In all things God works for the good of those who love Him,'" she reminded. "This is when you trust Him and believe He has something better in mind, something to help you succeed beyond anything you've imagined."

"Succeed how? By losing my dream or

losing my father?" He envied her assurance in God.

"The night Mrs. Purvis broke her arm and there was no other pianist to help with the choir, you said something." He couldn't look away from Doc's steady gaze, didn't want to. "You said 'Nothing is impossible for God.' Remember?"

"Yes. But—"

"It's Christmas, Brett. People thought a baby in a manger couldn't be the Messiah. They didn't believe a poor, unmarried girl could be His mother or that this baby would save people from their sins." Her smile spread until her whole face glowed. "The whole message of Christmas is God doing the impossible. Don't you think God, who keeps the universe spinning, can handle your father's illness *and* your dream of being a vet?"

Her words made him want to say yes, but he couldn't. Because nestled deep inside Brett was the reminder that God had taken

years to give him this opportunity and seconds to yank it away.

"Believe, Brett." Doc's other hand covered
their joined fingers, her grip strong. "Talk
to Clint. Most of all, believe that God loves
you and wants to give you the wishes of your
heart even more than you want them. He's
a good God."

Her phone broke the connection that zipped
between their locked gazes. Slowly Elizabeth removed her hand, took out her phone
and answered. Brett stiffened when her face
turned a sickly white. *What now?*

"I'll be right there," she whispered. She
swallowed and rose. "Zoey and Mrs. House
were in a car accident. They're at the hospital."

"I'll take you." Brett tossed some bills on
the table then hugged her against his side,
urging her toward his truck. Somehow Doc's
distress snapped him out of his self-centered
world. He had only one prayer in his head.
Please, Lord.

"I can't lose her." Elizabeth's frightened

voice was a ragged whisper. "I can't lose my daughter."

"Trust, Doc." Brett felt like a hypocrite as he wound his way through Christmas shoppers entering Snowflake for the town's gigantic bake sale. At the hospital, waiting for news, he texted his father, asking him to come in case Zoey needed him. And he prayed.

But his prayers seemed to hit a tin ceiling. One question taunted him.

Why was God allowing this?

"Zoey's going to be okay, Doc." Brett's voice seemed to penetrate a long, dark tunnel.

"Yes." Still Elizabeth couldn't stem her tears.

"Just a few bumps and bruises." Brett's arm circled her shoulders. It felt so right to settle against his side, to depend on him. "Sign the discharge papers."

"Don't cry, Mommy," Zoey whimpered. "I hurt an' Mrs. House has a bad cut but we'll be okay 'cause God looked after us."

"Yes, He did." The sight of her precious child wearing her goofy Christmas sweater and the silly mistletoe barrettes released Elizabeth's tension. She swept Zoey into her arms and held on. "I love you, sweetheart."

"I love you, too, Mommy. An' Brett, an' Mrs. Beasley, an' Clint, an' Mrs. House— too tight." She wiggled free of the embrace. "I'm hungry."

"So am I, kid." Clint clapped a hand on Brett's shoulder. "He's buying us pizza."

"Yum." Zoey slid her hand into Clint's before telling him how the rescue workers had freed them from their damaged car.

"I don't want to hear that." Elizabeth signed the papers, wishing Brett would hold her again. "I hope she doesn't have nightmares."

"She sounds like a normal kid describing her adventure." Something in his tone felt almost standoffish.

"Do you think we should go ahead with dress rehearsal tonight?" How could she breach the chilly wall between them?

"It's up to you." How unlike Brett not to

offer support or encouragement. Then she saw his eyes riveted on Clint.

"Have some faith."

"I don't think I have any left," he muttered so quietly she almost missed it.

"Then I'll have enough faith for both of us." Elizabeth ignored his coolness and hugged his side, using the excuse of the icy parking lot to grasp his hand. But when he pulled away as soon as they reached his truck, something inside her shrank.

Brett loved her. She knew that, sensed it in the way he treated her, comforted her, encouraged her. But he'd been bowled over by his father's illness. He would give up college because that was the kind of man he was. She wouldn't give up on him but she'd have to be patient while he worked it through.

Yet his silence through the meal, his lack of response to Zoey's teasing, the way he pulled away when she touched his arm— all of that worried Elizabeth. She loved this man. She dreamed of a future with him.

Maybe God didn't want that.

Sobered by that thought, she led the choir through their paces. Brett's timing with the sets was perfect. He moved quietly backstage, but he didn't smile, didn't even look at her, when she sang her solo. In fact, it was almost as if he wasn't there.

He drove her to retrieve her car, but aside from whispering that she'd be praying for him, Elizabeth didn't know what to do.

"Mommy, why is Brett sad?" Zoey asked when she'd been tucked into bed. "Is it 'cause his daddy's sick?"

"Where did you hear that?" She was shocked when Zoey said Clint had told her.

"Can't you make him better, Mommy?"

"I'm not his doctor, sweetie. But we'll all do our best to help him," she promised. "We'll pray for both Clint and Brett."

"I been prayin' for them a lot," Zoey said, snuggling down and closing her eyes. "An' for you, too, Mommy. This is gonna be the bestest Christmas."

"I hope so." But as she switched off the lamp and left the room, Elizabeth wondered if it might not be the hardest Christmas she'd ever gone through, especially if Brett couldn't find a way to love her.

Nothing is impossible for God.

She sat in her armchair staring at the Christmas tree Brett had delivered from his ranch. The lights, all red as per Zoey's wishes, blurred together as tears welled.

"I love him so much. But if that's not Your will for me then help me accept it. And please help the choir. I want the audience to see You. I want the choir to help everyone focus on the meaning of Christmas. For Your glory, not mine."

Elizabeth picked up her Bible and read the entire Christmas story. As she did, her heart filled with joy at the wonderful way God had chosen to give His precious gift to the world, in a stable with His creatures watching.

That made her think of Brett and his love of animals.

Help him, was all she could pray.

Chapter Ten

Snowflake's Christmas Eve kids' choir was spectacular. Perhaps not perfectly on key for every note, but that lack was made up in joyful zest. Clint was great, too. His readings drew hearts and minds to God.

Just before her solo, Elizabeth's heart took up double time when she caught Brett's gaze riveted on her. She steadied her breathing, swept a hand down her green dress and inhaled.

Tonight she was going to give the performance of her dreams. Tonight she'd finally erase the painful memories. She caught herself licking her lips as the intro played over the speakers and glanced at Brett once more.

Sing for God, sweetheart. I love you.

Brett's lips hadn't moved and yet as her gaze locked with his she felt his confidence reach across the room. Almost as if he was saying, "Believe what you sing."

I know that my Redeemer liveth.

It wasn't James's opinion, or Elizabeth's that mattered. It was God's and He didn't make failures. The knowledge sank heart-deep as Elizabeth hit her first notes bang on. She let herself feel young Mary's joy at the birth of this special baby. Faith bloomed as her voice soared, dipped, raced then slowed. And through it all she sensed Brett's support, encouraging her, willing her to let God use her voice to minister to the audience.

His unwavering support was like a barricade, shutting out all the negatives and sustaining her as she poured her heart and soul into the music, magnifying the Lord she served. Was anything too hard for God? Elizabeth trusted Him; she wanted others to know they could, too. She sang with her heart until the last note died away into the silence of the room. Then she bowed her head to worship her Lord.

A moment later the room exploded in applause. Elizabeth opened her eyes to find Brett watching her, his gorgeous eyes soft and melting, as they'd been on the first day they met. He threw her a big smile accompanied by a thumbs-up then turned to give Ernie the sign to slide in the next set.

She loved him so much.

"It's up to you, God. Please work it out."

Then Elizabeth lifted her hand and the children joyfully played their song with triangles tinkling as the room filled with Christmas joy.

The church hall echoed with congratulations on another successful Christmas Eve choir. Snowflakers enjoyed the treats loading down long festively decorated tables in the hall.

"Congratulations, Brett. Marvelous sets."

Brett deferred the praise to Doc and his dad, uncomfortable with being here, watching the woman he loved and feeling like his heart would break. He loved her but he wasn't right for her. She was a doctor. She'd been married to a surgeon and she had a voice that would break your heart. He'd never be more than a simple rancher.

How it hurt not to claim the love she'd said she felt for him.

Easing through the throng of people, Brett grabbed his coat and left. He walked through the snow, scuffing his boot toe against the drifts, knowing that he had to give up college. He had no other choice. His dreams, his goals, his plans—he had to let them all go no matter how much it hurt. He'd hoped that attaining a college degree would somehow make him more suitable for Elizabeth. Truth was, it wouldn't.

Clint's health was center stage now. The "someday" Brett had dreamed of for so long was never going to happen. It was time, past time, to accept that. He was and always would be a simple rancher.

It hurt desperately to face that but Brett couldn't change his mind. This afternoon he and his dad had talked openly about Clint's diagnosis. Then they'd met with his doctor, who assured them that the road ahead wouldn't be easy, but that Clint's cancer was treatable.

Okay, the dream was dead. But even though he was staying in Snowflake, it didn't change his future with Elizabeth. But, oh, how much better, how much easier it would be to accept losing his dream if Doc was by his side.

Impossible.

So how could Brett go on? How could he come to town, to church, see her and Zoey and hide his longing to love and be loved? Doc deserved so much more than him.

Brett peered into the night sky, his soul searching for a ray of—hope?

You love her. And she loves you. She told you so.

Yes, Doc had said that. But then she'd left it up to him. His choice.

His choice! Suddenly Brett's viewpoint shifted. Nothing was the way he'd planned. But maybe it could be better than he imagined. Maybe the only barrier to his happiness with Elizabeth was him and his certainty that she wanted more than he could give. Yet Doc had never said that. She'd said she loved him, loved the way he trusted God.

A light clicked on.

Idiot! Filled with shame and remorse, Brett bowed his head and apologized to God for trying to be in control.

"You are the King of my world. Who am I to tell You how my life should be?" He spoke the truth and felt stronger. "You brought Elizabeth and Zoey here. You put love into both our hearts. I will trust that You intended for us to be together. Please lead and guide us."

Brett studied the brightly lit church. In about half an hour the place would start emptying and families would gather around for the traditional Christmas Eve tree lighting.

Then they'd go home to spend Christmas Eve with their families.

"I'm going to need some help here, God." Brett went to find his father.

Amid congratulations Elizabeth searched for Brett. He wasn't there. Clint had left to pick up Mrs. Beasley so Elizabeth could give her to Zoey tonight. Her daughter would be ecstatic but Elizabeth felt deflated. It was Brett's voice she longed to hear, he who filled her heart, his arms she wished for. It was hard to feel joy but she'd vowed to trust her Heavenly Father no matter what.

To bolster that trust she slipped into the sanctuary and spent a few moments pouring out her heart to God, thanking Him for tonight's success, begging Him to sustain her still. Thus restored she slipped on her coat and stepped outside to join Zoey and her friends gathered around the tree.

"I thought you'd probably forgotten our tradition. Congratulations on your success tonight, Doc."

Joy exploded inside her at Brett's low mur-mur. He handed her an unlit candle, his smile turning her knees to jelly. Her happiness knew no bounds when he drew her against his side.

"Care to share one of my favorite Snow-flake traditions?" he asked with a grin.

"You say that about all of them," she teased, loving the glimmer of fun in his dark eyes.

"Because they are." His gaze held hers until she had to look away.

Someone lit the first candle and the flame was passed to others. As Brett lit hers then Zoey's, Elizabeth felt blessed. It was just a candle, but its flickering light seemed like a promise from God. A sign of hope. She joined the voices softly singing "Silent Night." Then, just before the last notes died away, the tree bloomed with light.

"Merry Christmas, Mommy," Zoey chirped.

"Merry Christmas, darling."

"Merry Christmas, Doc. Zoey." Brett echoed the wishes sent from person to person.

"Merry Christmas," Elizabeth returned.

His hand held hers, keeping her close until the crowd had extinguished their candles then quietly drifted away. She saw Pastor Bill coax Zoey aside. Finally she and Brett stood alone, bathed in the tree lights. She waited, but for what?

"I got a Christmas gift tonight, Doc." Brett's hand released hers to slide around her waist. "God showed me life is what I choose to make it. I choose to stay here in Snowflake until God says different. I belong with you. I love you, Elizabeth."

Dazed, Elizabeth flung her arms around him and kissed him in delight. Zoey wasn't the only Kendall who would get her Christmas wish.

"I love you, too, darling Brett." She leaned back to stare into his handsome face. "I don't know what the future holds, but I do know that if we trust God, He will always give us the best gifts."

"Will you marry me?" he asked.

"Yes." She reveled in his surprise, his embrace and the sweet touch of his lips against hers.

"This is a ring my dad bought for my mom. She left before he could give it to her. But he bought it with love and I thought it could become a tradition—" He stopped, obviously uncertain.

"It's beautiful, Brett. I accept. Will you put it on?"

He did and kissed it in place until Zoey's giggles broke the silent night.

"Zoey, come here. I want to marry your mom," Brett said. "Is that okay with you?"

"Does it mean I'm getting a daddy for Christmas?" When Brett nodded she whooped for joy. "It's okay with me, but I gotta ask Mrs. Beasley."

"You can ask her right now, honey." Elizabeth walked over to Clint, who appeared from the side of the church, tromping through the snow, grumbling. She kissed his cheek, whispered thank-you, then lifted the puppy from inside his coat and presented it to her daughter. "Merry Christmas, darling."

"Oh, thank you, Mommy." Zoey scooped the puppy into her arms and pressed a kiss against its nose. "Hey, CC, I get a puppy an' a daddy for Christmas." Then she frowned at Brett. "Don't you gotta ask your dad if you can marry my mommy?"

"Ask me?" Clint scoffed. "I had the idea ages ago, kid. I've got lots of other ones, too. But at the moment my best idea is sitting around a fire drying my feet and eating those Christmas cookies you and I decorated."

"Is that a tradition?" Elizabeth asked her beloved, tongue in cheek.

"It is now. So's this." Brett kissed Elizabeth. "The first of many traditions we'll share."

Elizabeth's phone beeped. "Here's another. I have to deliver a baby tonight."

"I'll drive you." Brett threaded his fingers through hers. "Dad, can you take Zoey home? I'll wait and bring Doc later."

"It could take a while," Elizabeth reminded.

"I will always wait for you for as long as it takes," he promised.

Epilogue

One year later
Snowflake's Christmas Eve Kids' Choir
Service

Elizabeth sustained the last note as long as she could then let silence fall on the hushed congregation, hoping no one would notice that she'd cut it short. Another contraction gripped her abdomen as applause rang out. She motioned for the children to bow, fingers twining around her music stand for support while she waited for it to end.

The stand gave way under pressure and a loud crash echoed through the sanctuary as

Maisie Jones banged three discordant notes on the piano. Everyone stared.

"You all just help yourself to the lunch in the hall now," the pianist ordered in an officious tone. "Doc has an emergency." With that pronouncement, she strode to Elizabeth, wrapped a strong arm around her waist and shepherded her off stage. "Lean on me, Dr. Liz."

"Can you please find my husband?"

"Right here, Doc." Brett appeared beside her, his handsome face frowning. "What's wrong?"

"She needs to get to the hospital. Now." Maisie grinned. "My guess is she's been havin' pains since I hit the third bar of music."

"Sweetheart, why didn't you stop?" Brett slipped his arm around her waist, pausing until she let go of her pent-up breath before wrapping her coat around her. "Pretty close together, aren't they?" he asked worriedly.

"Yes, but I am not delivering in church. Thanks, Maisie." She waved a hand then stepped forward, gripped Brett's fingers, closed her eyes and groaned. "Oh, boy."

"Better move, son." Maisie held open the side door, grinning as Brett swept his wife into his arms and carried her outside. "Don't drop her," she warned.

"As if!" he snorted indignantly then grinned when he saw his dad waiting with the truck running. "Thanks, Dad."

Once he and Doc were inside Clint headed for the hospital. Maisie must have called the police chief because he led the way, lights flashing.

"Great town, Snowflake. Everybody pitches in when they're needed." Clint pulled in under the emergency awning. "Love you, Elizabeth," he said as his son eased her from the car.

"Love you, to—" Her voice died away as she continued her breathing exercises.

"I'll look after Zoey." Clint's smile was huge. "I'm gonna be a grandfather again."

"We love you, Dad."

"It's mutual, son."

"There, Brett." Pointing to a nurse with a wheelchair waiting, Elizabeth squeezed her hubby's hand and held on, her gaze meeting his in a union of love and commitment. "Ready, Daddy?"

Brett's nervous nod made her smile.

After that everything moved at lightning speed, though it seemed only moments later that their son was born.

And then their daughter.

"They're not as pretty as my dollies." Zoey's freckled nose wrinkled early Christmas morning.

"They're beautiful. So's your mother." Brett gazed at Doc, heart overflowing. "I am blessed. A year ago I had no idea this could happen."

"Nothing is impossible for God," Doc reminded him. Then she frowned. "Is that mistletoe in your pocket, honey?"

Brett nodded then winked at Zoey, who held it over her mom's head.

"Merry Christmas, darling." He kissed her tenderly.

"Yes, but mistletoe?" Elizabeth looked toward Clint, who grinned at Zoey.

"Daddy thought the babies'd be boys. He was gonna name 'em Misa and Toby." Zoey's laugh tinkled. "Get it? Mistletoe?"

Brett chuckled at Elizabeth's groan.

"Come on, Zoey. Let's go have some Christmas hot chocolate at home and make a new tradition." Clint snuggled the little girl's hand in his. "Merry Christmas, kids."

"Merry Christmas." Brett smiled at Doc. "I like our traditions."

"Me, too." Misty-eyed, Elizabeth reached out. "I need to hold them again."

Brett placed one child in each arm and savored the sight.

"Thank you for my lovely Christmas gifts, sweetheart. I have everything any man could want."

"We both do. Clint sailed through therapy and is doing great. My clinic work is fantastic and soon you'll begin your second year of distance studies toward your degree." Doc motioned him to sit next to her. "My Christmas Eve cowboy. Isn't trusting God's plan the best way?"

"Perfect." Brett bent to kiss her. Through the window he saw his dad and Zoey throwing snowballs at each other. "Absolutely perfect."

* * * * *

*Don't miss these other stories
from Lois Richer:*

*THE RANCHER'S FAMILY WISH
HER CHRISTMAS FAMILY WISH
THE COWBOY'S EASTER FAMILY WISH
THE TWINS' FAMILY WISH*

Available now from Love Inspired!

*Find more great reads at
www.LoveInspired.com*

Dear Reader,

I'm a self-confessed Christmas-a-holic. I love the songs, the decorations, the gift-giving and the food. But mostly I love traditions like my mom's delicious chicken pot pie, driving through town to see the lights and taking just the right picture for our annual Christmas card.

Christmas is a time to expect the unexpected. Like a baby in a manger and shepherds seeing angels and rich men following a star. It's okay to be childlike at Christmas, to let your heart bask in heaven-sent love. Why don't we make Christmas happen all year long?

This Christmas may you know boundless love, immeasurable peace and uncontainable joy. Most of all, may you feel the Father's love sent, as Zoey would say, 'specially from His heart to yours.

Merry Christmas to all.